Love Without Reservations

A Love in Mission City Novella

GABBI GREY

Edits by ELF

Cover by Jo Clement

Dedication

Michele

Lisa

Contents

Chapter One

Noel

S howing up at some random dude's house to track down my wayward sister wasn't the craziest thing I'd done to try to keep her safe—but pretty damn close.

As I pounded on the door of the two-story house with white siding, I questioned my life choices. What was I doing in Cataluma, California? Why was I so obsessed about making sure Kendra didn't make yet another mistake? How could I possibly persuade her to come back to Canada with me? She'd made a commitment to our father that she'd leave in two day's time—Monday morning—but I had zero faith in that. Our father suggested she was interested in this small town. And given she'd not answered any of my many-dozen messages, I really needed to have my head examined for showing up here unannounced.

If you told her that you were coming, she might've left.

Yes, well, that was a distinct possibility.

Again, I pounded.

"Young man."

I spun.

An older woman stood just a few feet behind me. She wore a flowered dress, a pillbox hat, carried a fabric purse and...wore slippers.

Unsure how to react, I stepped forward. "Yes, ma'am."

"You may call me Mrs. Jensen."

"Yes, ma'am."

She scowled.

"Yes, Mrs. Jensen. And how are you this evening?"

Eyes narrowed. "You're here to see the Fernandez boy?"

A myriad of responses came to mind, but I figured I'd go for simple. "Yes, do you know where he is?"

She scowled. "At the dance. With that floozy."

Inwardly, I winced. Odds were, the woman was discussing my sister. At least I assumed that—given Kendra's Harley sat in the driveway. "Do you know the floozy's name?"

"As if." Another scowl. Then she leaned in, as if to impart some great secret. "She's one of many. Javier's a philanderer. A different woman each week."

Okay, I was really not liking this Javier guy. Worry for Kendra's safety clawed at my throat. Maybe this guy was a serial killer—and the women he brought home were never heard from again. Or maybe he got them knocked up and then abandoned them. Or maybe—

"When you see Javier, tell him I'm disappointed. I knew his father. Good man. His mother...well, the less said about her, the better."

I wasn't even going to try to interpret that statement. "So, which way to the dance?"

She pointed, and I tried to envision the town in my mind. Likely I'd need to go back to the main road and... What? Surely there'd be signs to this Strawberry Festival. My keys sat heavy in my hand, and I itched to race over there, but consideration had me offering my arm. "May I help you home?"

"Aren't you just a gentleman? Yes, that's my house." She pointed across the street.

She linked her arm with mine, and we walked across to her home.

Despite my impatience, I waited until she was inside and the lock clicked into place. Then I spun, strode across the street, and got into my car. I made my way back to Prospector's Row and took a gamble as to the probable location of the dance. Soon enough, I came across a park. At the very edge of a large lot, a car was pulling away.

I eased into the spot. My suitcases were in the back of my SUV, so I locked it, hoped no thieves cased the lot, and headed toward the noise.

As I approached, I spotted two men standing on a stage. One was tall and what my mother would've said was distinguished. His tuxedo seemed incongruous with everyone else's shorts, khakis, or jeans. The other man was about the same height but younger. Closer in age to me, if I had to guess. As they conferred at the microphone, I surveyed the crowd.

Kendra.

She stood with a couple. The man and woman held hands, so probably a couple.

I approached the group quietly, not wanting to make a scene. I grabbed Kendra's arm and started pulling her.

She whirled and took a fighter's stance, obviously prepared to do battle. Jesus, I shouldn't have snuck up on her. And if we started fighting here, at this...event...it'd look bad. But I needed to get her out of here and get us back on the road as soon as possible.

"Noel?"

Her face registered shock, given her slack-jawed expression and the narrowing of her blue eyes.

Eyes so like my own.

"Hey, let go of her." The tall man glowered at me.

My first reaction was to tell the guy to fuck right off. This was *my* wayward sister, and *I* knew what was best for her. Anger simmered within me, and my heartrate increased.

"Hey." A shorter woman with curly hair came up to me and got right into my face. She even had the temerity to poke her finger at my chest. "You let her go."

I wanted to swat her hand away like I'd swat a mosquito, but the guy was by her side and, clearly, they came as a unit. And I'd have to risk letting go of Kendra, and that so wasn't happening.

"Yeah." A random voice from the crowd carried. "Let her go."

Damn, this is getting out of hand. Fuck.

More people chorused in and, suddenly, I considered what this looked like. These people didn't know me. Didn't know my relationship to Kendra. Didn't know I had only her best interests at heart. I didn't spot any law enforcement, but that didn't mean they weren't around. Reluctantly, I released my grip on her arm. "Look, you need to come with me."

"I don't *need* to do anything." Kendra crossed her arms and rubbed the spot where I'd grabbed her.

For show, or had I really hurt her? Yet another damn.

"What the fuck are you doing here, Noel?"

"You know this guy?" The dude with long hair looked back and forth between the two of us. I wouldn't put it past him to step in. I'd bet I could take him, but likely the crowd would take his side and, just as likely, I'd get arrested.

The nosy woman with the dude squinted. "You're siblings."

Kendra's hair was lighter than mine, and her eye color wasn't obvious in the fading light, but certain similarities existed between the two of us. Not to mention the Barker nose as well as the fact she was so tall, we were able to see eye to eye. I had an inch or two on her, but that rarely meant anything.

"He's my brother, but I have no idea why he's here."

Jesus, was she really that dense? Or was she playing some kind of game? With my dear sister, it could go either way. "I'm here to get you. To stop you from making a huge mistake."

She tilted her head in that way that drove me nuts. Her way of saying *I'm going to play dumb.* The truth was that she wasn't dumb. Not by a long shot. Scatterbrained and flighty? Sure. Dumb? Not a chance.

"And what mistake would that be?"

God help me. "I find you shacked up with some guy—"

Her eyes flashed. "Jesus, Noel." Then a frown marred her brow. "How do you know about me and Javier?"

"Maybe the fact your phone is at his house. And he's a well-known player in town?"

The shorter lady demanded. "Who told you that?"

"His neighbor. A nice older woman who was only too happy to enlighten me about the string of women he's had come through his house." Although what the point was of this, I wasn't sure.

A bark of laughter escaped the woman. "You're talking about Mrs. Jensen. Lost her mind years ago. She only *thinks* she knows what all is going on. Heck, she thinks Sequoia's a woman because of his hair."

Sequoia. What kind of name was that? Undoubtedly some hippie California surfer dude. Although we weren't that close to the ocean.

Focus.

"She said—"

"You tracked my phone?" Kendra's high-pitched and indignant shout drew the attention of several onlookers.

Damn, a crowd was gathering to watch the show. "How the hell else was I going to find you? You tell our father you're in some town with a strawberry festival, and I find you've finally left your phone on long enough to track..." I'd put the software on the damn thing when I gave it to her as a gift—because she was forgetful and had lost several in the past. This one'd been damn expensive, and I wanted us to have a way to find it if she ever left it behind somewhere. I'd never foreseen using it to track her.

So you tell yourself.

"That sounds like stalking." Sequoia's brow knit. "Isn't that illegal?"

"I told her I installed the software when I bought her the phone." There, see? I could defend myself. Not that I should have to.

"You told me that was in case I lost it." Her anger hadn't diminished—if anything, it increased.

I put my hands on my hips. *This is getting us nowhere.* "You assumed. I never actually said—"

"Kendra?" Some guy barrelled through the crowd—the guy I'd spotted on the stage earlier.

Just great.

He came up behind her and stood so close that if she leaned back, she'd be flat against his chest.

Ah, so this was the dude. Javier Fernandez. He was taller than me by a couple of inches. But while he was wiry, I had a bit more heft. Even in the darkening night, his tanned skin was visible, and his eyes were almost black. Likely he had some kind of Latino or Hispanic heritage. I wasn't going to be derailed. "This the guy?"

"Who is this?"

Javier's voice carried what I assumed was supposed to be menace. I still believed I could take him. Just not him and Sequoia and whomever else might jump into the fray. Didn't put it past the woman with the tats and the dour expression not to jump in as well.

Why was I obsessing about fighting? I was a pacifist by nature. Maybe not like I assumed these hippie people to be, but I never fought. Even growing up, I'd defended people weaker than me, but always with words—never with deeds.

Kendra blinked. "This is my brother." She grabbed Javier's hand. Then she spun back to me. "And this is the man I love—Javier."

Jesus fucking Christ.

I staggered back a step.

Okay, flighty, fanciful, daydreamy, Kendra believed she was in love? She wasn't, of course. Apparently, she'd been in town all of four days, and people definitely didn't fall in love in just four days.

Goddammit, they've had sex.

I so did *not* want to think about my sister's sex life, but she tended to, uh, do it with guys quite quickly after meeting them.

She claimed she needed to know if they were sexually compatible because, otherwise, she wasn't wasting her time with them.

I bristled. "You've known him for how long?"

Javier pulled her back and wound his arms around her. "Time is irrelevant. We both know what we want."

Oh, great, two irresponsible people. Just what I need.

"She's a child, Javier." Did he not see? "Never finished university, never held down a proper job, never—"

"I know all that, and I don't give a shit." Javier wrapped his arms around her waist. "You have a different perspective. You're protective of her—which is great."

Kendra didn't appear pleased with that concession. She continued to scowl.

"You talk about time." I scowled right back. "She has to come back to Canada shortly, or she'll be in big trouble with the immigration authorities." Surely she'd figured this out by now. "There are rules."

I expected her to say *fuck the rules*, but she didn't. I hadn't done research on immigration, but my friend's parents came south for the winter, and they had to be back in Canada before the six-month mark or they risked pissing off both the American and Canadian authorities.

Kendra's lower lip stuck out. "You just don't want me to be happy."

Jesus, is she for real? "I've only ever wanted your happiness, Kendra. But I don't think running away—"

"Maybe I was running to something."

I wanted to demand to know what. This guy? She hadn't known him. Or had she? Maybe they'd hooked up on some dating app. Or maybe he'd lured her here with promises he never intended to keep.

Javier pressed a kiss to her temple. "We'll find a way to make this work."

"Don't make promises you can't keep." I was ready to lose my ever-loving shit.

"Go home, Noel. Go back to Canada and leave me alone."

I moved toward her. She appeared momentarily startled, but she didn't look like she was going to back down.

Javier glared.

"Hey, how's everyone doing?"

As a group, everyone turned to face another dude.

The guy wore jeans and a crewneck, light-blue shirt. His eyes were almost as black as his dark skin. He was my height, with broad shoulders and a firm stance. Him, I would've noticed—even without the friendly intervention.

"None of your business." Even as I said the words, I felt compelled to hold the guy's gaze. Drop-dead gorgeous with kind eyes.

You're obsessing over his eyes? Really?

The man spoke. "Look, why don't you come with me? We can take a walk."

He's serious? "I'm talking with my sister."

"Who isn't in the mood to listen." The guy met my gaze and held it. "But she'll be here tomorrow and, when everyone's cooled off, you can have a rational conversation."

"I'm not letting this go." I pitched my voice low so only Kendra and Javier could hear. I probably didn't need to add so much menace—but I needed them to know I was serious.

"I'm not letting her go." Javier gripped her tighter.

"I'm not leaving." Her chin jutted in *that way*. Boy, I was in for a world of hurt.

The newcomer put a gentle hand on my arm.

After what felt like a moment that spun out forever, I acquiesced and followed him away.

The music started up, but it quickly faded as we walked away from the park.

What have I gotten myself into?

Chapter Two

Aaron

I'd lived in Cataluma my entire life. Occasionally trouble would crop up at the Strawberry Festival—usually when some out-of-towner over imbibed. Well, there was the time the Watsons and the Wainwrights took their feud public and had a showdown at the Saturday-night dance. Jeremy Watson and Isabel Wainwright declared their love and had threatened a Romeo and Juliet if their families didn't reconcile their, frankly, petty differences.

That'd been back in eighty-six. I'd been knee high to a grasshopper and hadn't understood the fuss.

I'd grown up a lot in the intervening thirty-six years.

Witnessing Kendra and Javier was like watching the Wainwright/Watson feud all over again. I hoped the conflict resolved itself much as the old one had—Isabel and Jeremy had five children, two grandchildren, and lived happy lives.

As I guided Kendra's protective older brother out of the park and toward the cars, I held my tongue. Guy probably thought I was an interfering busybody.

He wasn't wrong.

I didn't like conflict. I'd grown up with too much of it in my household, and I'd sworn never to let it back into my life. Sure, being the proprietor of the Cataluma Inn meant dealing with issues—unhappy guests, disgruntled staff, and other stuff. But I'd learned to let skirmishes roll off my back. I was stronger than that.

"You can let go of me."

The man's softly spoken words alerted me to the fact I still held his elbow. I'd led him—gently. And he'd followed—willingly.

With some reluctance, I let him go. "What's your name?" I wracked my brain, but couldn't remember it.

He halted under a streetlamp. "You didn't hear everything?"

I shook my head. "Only the last few words."

"Then why'd you step in?"

Good question.

"Just seemed to me that I could help. You attracted quite a crowd, and I didn't figure you were a guy who liked the spotlight." That might've been a stretch, but I had a gut-deep feeling about this guy.

He cleared his throat. "Noel. Noel Barker. And you're right—I don't like causing scenes. Yet, when it comes to Kendra..."

Ah. "I have a much-younger brother. I love Trey, but he's been a handful."

"How much younger?"

"Twenty-two years or so. Theoretically, he's my half-brother, but I helped raise him, and I see him as my flesh and blood. Labels don't mean anything to me."

"But you understand younger siblings." He glanced over his shoulder. "I've only ever wanted what was best for her." Turning back, he met my gaze. "I have to find a place for the night. Even if I wasn't planning to see Kendra tomorrow—which I am—I've been on the road since dawn."

"You've come from Canada?"

"Yeah, I left first thing yesterday morning."

I cocked my head.

He winced. "Yeah, I tracked her phone. Didn't have a choice. She's always losing it—"

"And you thought she'd lost it in Cataluma, and you'd come all the way down to get it?"

"Well, she confirmed to my father that she was in a small town with a strawberry festival. Between this hit on the phone and Cataluma's town website, I knew I'd struck gold. I just didn't know if she'd still be here. I stopped for a brief respite last night in Eugene, Oregon, but came straight through this morning."

Good God, that was a long trip. Canada to Cataluma was over a thousand miles. "You need a place to rest."

"Yeah." On cue, he yawned. "I don't suppose you know a place to stay?"

"Well, we only have a few shared accommodations in town, and they're all full up. This weekend is the busiest of the year in Cataluma. Well, Christmas is hopping as well." I hesitated.

He nodded encouragingly.

"I own the only inn in town."

"Great—"

"We're full."

For just an instant, I caught the despair in his eyes. In his down-turned mouth. "That's all right—I can sleep in the back of my SUV."

No way was I letting him do that.

Boldly, I touched his arm. "I have a spare bed in my apartment at the inn."

"You live on-site?"

I nodded. "Yeah, I did some renovations when I took over. I liked the idea of living on-site and being able to deal with problems as they crop up."

"That doesn't sound like a healthy work/life balance."

He had a point.

"Cataluma Inn is my life."

"No wife, or girlfriend, or..." He winced and rubbed his forehead. "Damn, I'm so fucking tired."

"Let's get your car and drive back to the inn—it's at the other end of town."

He pointed to a nice black SUV with British Columbia license plates.

"You don't mind catching a lift with me?"

I snorted. "I think I can handle my own if you decide to get frisky." Of course, I wouldn't mind if he got fresh with me. I was in what I hoped was the middle of a long dry spell. A spell I hoped would end soon.

Getting into the vehicle, I sank into the luxury of the seat.

He hopped in, closed the door, and put the key in the engine.

"Wow, are these heated seats?"

"It's a Canadian thing."

"Cool. We have them in the States too, but my brother's car doesn't."

He started the engine.

As he pulled back onto the street, I casually mentioned, "It would be a boyfriend. Or husband."

Even while driving, he shot me a look. Quickly, his eyes were back on the road, but I'd caught it. The look.

"Uh, yeah, cool."

"The parking lot for the inn is up ahead." I pointed.

He turned in and found the last parking spot. Anyone who came afterward could park on the street until nine a.m.

After shutting off the engine, he sat for a moment—keys in his hand. Finally, he cut me a glance. "I'm gay too."

I'd been pretty darn sure, but never would have presumed. That'd gotten me into trouble a time or two. "Then we're good." I gave him a reassuring smile before we both alighted the vehicle.

He popped the trunk and snagged a suitcase.

After he closed and locked the SUV with the remote, we headed into the inn.

As always, a sense of well-being invaded my senses. The dining room was full to bursting with people here for the festival but who weren't interested in the dance. I spotted a few friends I knew, but opted not to go and chat. Instead, I led Noel up the stairs all the way to the third floor. I'd renovated two large suites into an apartment. The loss of revenue was worth it for all the problems I'd resolved over the years by being here. My staff knew to only disturb me when something urgent arose. I hired—and retained—top talent. I was regularly voted one of the best employers in town. And I didn't even have to bribe my employees to vote for me.

I unlocked the door and held it open for my guest to enter.

He did, although clearly with some trepidation, slowly stepping in.

What was he expecting?

I kept my place as neat as could be, and housekeeping came by twice a week—including this morning—to keep the space in excellent order. After locking the door, I dropped my keys on a table strategically placed by the front door. I never had to worry about finding the fuckers.

As I advanced into the room, I pointed to one door. "Bathroom." Then to the other. "Bedroom."

"Uh…" He looked around the room with a furrow in his brow.

I'd opted for a large, airy, open space. I had a dining room, an alcove with my computer equipment, and a large living room with a decent-sized television. I pointed to the sectional. "Pullout couch. I'm happy to take it and give you the nice comfortable bed with the ergonomic mattress."

"Oh no, I couldn't." His expression was all earnestness.

"My grandmother used to sleep there when she came to visit. The couch is very comfortable."

"Great, so I can sleep on it." He pressed a hand to his stomach.

"Let me order us some food. Any preferences? You allergic to anything? Vegetarian or something?"

"Uh, no to all those questions. I'll eat anything at this point." He swayed a little.

Ah, the adrenaline was wearing off.

"Why don't you sit while I order us some burgers? That'll be quickest. Any toppings you don't like?"

He shook his head. Then pointed to the bathroom.

"Of course. Take your time."

After a moment, he moved toward the alcove where he located some floor space. He opened his suitcase, grabbed what I assumed was his mess kit, and headed into the bathroom.

I snagged my cell phone.

Within moments, Cecilia answered. "What's up, boss?

My ever-efficient front desk clerk refused to call me by my first name.

"I'd like to place an order. Two steak burgers, an order of sweet potato fries, one of regular fries, a side of Caesar salad, and two slices of cheesecake with fresh strawberries."

The pause was momentary, but it was there.

"Yes, Cecilia, two."

"Of course." She rushed the words. "I'll have that cooked up in a jiffy and delivered to you right away. Anything else?"

"Nope, that's great." I hung up.

Noel emerged from the bathroom. His spikey, very dark-blond hair appeared more tamed, and his blue eyes shone brighter than before. He seemed...calmer.

"Everything okay?"

Slowly, he nodded. "Yeah, thanks." He headed over to his suitcase.

When he started to close it, I waylaid him. "You can keep it open. I don't use the computer much—I have a small office downstairs where I spend most of my working time."

He glanced over at the very expensive computer and large screen.

"Well, I might do some gaming."

A knowing smile spread across his face. "I've done that a time or two as well." He indicated his suitcase. "Would you mind if I change into something more comfortable?"

I'd wondered about his navy linen trousers, crisp white shirt that, admittedly, was looking a little wilted, and his loafers. "Trying to make a good first impression?"

He slowly nodded. "I thought if I came here wearing a suit that I might be taken more seriously." A bark of a laugh. "Joke was on me."

"I take you seriously."

His gaze shot to mine. He licked his lips.

As we held gazes, I took a moment to appreciate the view. Clearly, it'd been a day or two since he'd shaved—the scruff was sexy. He was about my height. Usually, I preferred guys taller than me, but I liked how he had some definition. Did he work out? I wouldn't ask outright, but I'd ferret out a response. I liked guys who took care of themselves, but beefy didn't work for me either.

"Pajamas." His hoarse voice hit me right in the gut and skittered downward.

"Of course. I'm going to head downstairs to get our food." Cecelia could run it up, but I liked to do things myself. And pausing to reflect on the significance of the moment seemed like a good idea.

We parted ways, and I headed downstairs. The food wasn't ready, but I was happy to wait. I wandered among the tables, chatting with friends and guests who wanted my attention. Compliments abounded, and I felt no small amount of pride at what I'd created. When I arrived, the inn had good bones, but'd needed a major makeover. I'd brought it out of the seventies and into the current century. Then I'd embarked on creating a restaurant that offered the finest dining in Cataluma.

I was pretty pleased with the result.

When the food was ready, I headed back upstairs.

Noel sat at the dining room table, looking exhausted.

"Eat up. We can deal with everything else in the morning." I wasn't sure what *everything else* was, but we'd figure it out. Although I barely knew her, I'd come to care for Kendra. And despite barely knowing him, I was coming to care for Noel.

"What am I going to do about Kendra?" Despair laced his voice as he ate another sweet potato fry.

"I don't know that you have to do anything—she's a grown woman. If she decides to stay in Cataluma, I'm certain we can help her find a way to navigate that."

"She doesn't know what's best for her. She's impetuous and reckless."

Gently, I placed my hand on Noel's arm.

His gaze met mine.

"I understand you want what's best for your sister. But maybe it's time to let go."

He bit his lower lip. "I don't know if I can."

"Well, you might not have a choice. We'll see how things play out."

I didn't want him to leave Cataluma, but he had a life in Canada. Whether Kendra stayed in California was up to her—and the immigration authorities.

We resumed eating, and by the time we finished the cheesecake, Noel could barely keep his eyes open.

I made the pullout couch up and coaxed him under the covers. Before I even turned out the light, he was gone.

What have you gotten yourself into?

I wasn't sure...but I'd go along for the ride just to find out.

Chapter Three

Noel

When I awoke after twelve straight hours of sleep, I discovered a breakfast platter with instructions on how to heat up the eggs and bacon in the microwave. I raced to the bathroom and was back at the table within moments. After I'd reheated the coffee as well, I sat. I was starving and ate everything on the plate and even eyed the parsley.

Nah. I could always get more food later.

As I was cleaning up the dishes, I caught sight of a note from Aaron, informing me he was downstairs if I needed him, but otherwise to enjoy myself. Oh, and a key. Perfect. I organized my clothes for the day—khaki pants and another cotton, button-down shirt. This one, though, wasn't a dress shirt. I rolled up the sleeves in an attempt to look more casual.

Glancing in the mirror in the bathroom, I wasn't convinced I had the right effect. Still, worth the effort. I brushed my teeth, tidied away the suitcase, locked the door, and headed downstairs.

A nice-looking older gentleman sat at the registration desk. He offered me a wide-grin. "And how are you this morning?" His nametag read Jason.

"I'm doing well, Jason." I gazed around.

"Are you looking for someone? Or might you be interested in a brunch? The restaurant serves a mean eggs Benedict."

Tempted as I was to inquire after Aaron, I didn't want to disturb him—I'd been enough of a disruption already. "I think I'm going to head out for a walk."

"Oh, well, you need to attend the festival. Last day."

His kind eyes shone with enthusiasm. Apparently, this was an entire-town event.

"I'll do that." I headed outside and made my way down the street. I passed various shops and a café. Then I spotted High Sierra. A marijuana store.

An unrelated and odd thought struck me. I hadn't looked into Javier Fernandez. I'd been so tired last night that it hadn't even been a possibility. After yanking my phone out of my back pocket, I sat on a bench. Grateful I'd worn my sunglasses, I started a google search. My out-of-country data charges would be horrendous, but that didn't matter. I needed to find out more about this guy my sister had the hots for.

The search took three seconds to return results, and at the top, was High Sierra. I didn't have any explanation why I'd looked at the store and thought about Javier. In fact, if I was brutally honest, I'd have pegged the dude with the long hair from last night. Sequoia? God, such a California name.

You're being pretentious.

Okay, so I was. I dealt with all kinds of people in my business—including people who didn't dress in business attire—and I always withheld my judgement until I got to know them. I'd passed a snap judgement on one guy—Spike—and that'd nearly cost me a contract. Because he was a motorcycle mechanic, I hadn't figured he'd have a head for business or see the importance of marketing. Fortunately, he hadn't held my poor attitude against me and, on our second meeting, had hired me to do promotions for his shop. He liked that I was LGBTQ-friendly. Probably helped that he was gay, but he also expected great things from me.

I'd delivered.

Now he was a friend.

When I first met him, thanks to Kendra's burning need to buy a Harley, I'd noticed him in a *you're cute* way. Clearly, though, he was enamored with his next-door neighbor, Dickens. That guy owned the bookstore in Mission City and also employed my services. I didn't care why people hired me—only that they did.

I tucked my phone away and resumed my journey to the festival. I had high hopes of running into Kendra. If I didn't, then I'd head back to Javier's house. Or maybe to High Sierra. Except I didn't want a scene at the man's place of business. I was pissed—but not that pissed.

Passing various stalls, I kept an eye out for a tall, blonde woman. Kendra stood out in most crowds—because of her hair and for her height.

A raucous crowd caught my attention.

I called myself all kinds of crazy and stupid—a word my mother abhorred—as I made my way to a field where apparently everyone was playing flag football. I enjoyed hiking—whenever I got the chance—and running when I was home in Mission City. Occasionally

I hiked with friends, but I often went alone—sticking to trails where there'd be other people in case I got into trouble. I never did, though. I was safety-conscious.

Truthfully, I didn't consider any form of football safe.

Aha. Kendra stood off to one side, next to a smaller blonde woman who could've, honestly, been her older sister. Their resemblance was striking.

I made a beeline toward them.

Kendra spotted me and offered a tentative wave.

Damn, so she wasn't going to make this easy. As I approached, I nodded to the blonde woman and beckoned Kendra to the side.

She didn't look pleased, with her brow knitting, but she followed.

"Have you come to your senses? We can put your bike on a freight train, and you can drive home with me. I would've brought an SUV big enough to haul a bike, but, apparently, they don't make one big enough to fit a Harley—even the women's version."

I tried to keep the derision out of my voice. I didn't have an issue with her riding because she was a woman—I had an issue with anyone who was crazy enough to get on a motorcycle. I didn't want to think of how far she'd driven over the past few months.

My aunt Lucille used to call riders of those horrible things *organ donors*. I couldn't fault her logic.

"Jesus, Noel. You think I'm going to trust my baby to some shipping company? Are you out of your fucking mind?" She cast a glance at the woman standing a few feet away.

The woman who wasn't even pretending not to eavesdrop.

"Fine. We can drive together. I'll go in front. If we leave today—"

"Oh my God, Noel, are you listening to yourself? I'm not leaving Cataluma."

She almost said *ever*. The word was on the tip of her tongue and blazing in her eyes.

I knew it. Deep inside, I knew her as well. If she was going to be stubborn about this, there was likely little I could do.

I caught sight of Javier abandoning the game and heading our way.

Kendra drew me back into the argument. "Goddammit, Noel, I told you to butt out. This is *my* life. If I want to fuck it up, that's up to me."

Ignoring Javier, I focused on my wayward sister. "I don't want you to wind up in an American jail, Kendra. That's not something to be taken lightly."

"Well...I found a solution to that."

Do I really want to know? Probably not, but she was likely to tell me, anyway. "And that would be? Going to petition the government to allow you to stay?"

"No." Kendra placed her hands on her hips. "Javier and I are going to get married."

What? I couldn't have heard her correctly and yet, instinctively, I knew I had. God, of all the impetuous, reckless, stupid—

Heat rose in my cheeks as anger boiled over.

Javier snagged Kendra and put an arm around her waist.

"You can't." I sputtered the denial.

"Oh, I can," she countered.

"The authorities will question it—all of it. You've only just met." Did she not see how this would look? Any immigration agent worth their salt would question the rapidity of the marriage. Wonder about the authenticity of it. And, if they decided Kendra'd lied, she could face consequences beyond just deportation. Might she face criminal charges? Jesus, I just didn't know.

"And maybe I'll have to go back to Canada while things get sorted, but I'm betting there's an excellent lawyer in town who'll help me get all my paperwork in order." She jutted her chin out.

For an instant, I considered violence. I would never, of course, but my sister knew how to push all my buttons.

"There is."

I spun to find Aaron joining us. I hadn't even seen him approach. Of course, I didn't want him to see me this way.

"Nice to see you again, Miss Barker."

"It's Kendra." She offered Aaron a warm smile.

Aaron obviously knew that. What was going on?

"I was just explaining to your brother that you might find a way to stay in Cataluma, if you set your mind to it."

What he neglected to mention—to his credit—was that I'd slipped away from the inn without finishing our conversation from last night. We'd talked about something, but I'd been so exhausted, I barely remembered anything.

"Well, obviously that discussion went well." Typical Kendra sarcasm.

Aaron turned toward me. "I thought we'd reached an understanding."

Finally, for the first time, I met his gaze. Damn, was I blushing? No, just the heat from the anger that hadn't entirely dissipated.

Show you can be a reasonable guy. "You...made some valid points." I nodded toward Javier. "I just don't know if he's good enough for her."

Javier's brown eyes shot daggers. "You don't know me—"

Kendra slashed her hand through the air. "That better not be racism."

What? Holy shit. And she thinks I'm going there? "I'd never...I..." I sputtered. "It's just, you know, he owns a pot shop. He probably—"

This time, Javier slashed his hand through the air. "Maybe in the past that would be an issue, but not these days. I run a respectable establishment and follow all the laws." He turned to Kendra. "I'll marry you. I'd be honored to be yours. And to call you mine. But your brother's right—we need to consult a lawyer. We can't do this half-assed."

So this hadn't been discussed previously? This was all spur of the moment? Because of me and my presence?

Shit.

To my utter shock, Javier dropped to one knee.

Kendra gasped.

Several people tittered.

The woman from last night snickered.

I growled.

Aaron chuckled.

Turning, I glared at him.

He held up his hands.

God, I found it hard to stay mad at the man.

"I don't have a ring." Javier snagged Kendra's hand.

"I don't need a ring."

To my shock, she dropped to one knee as well.

Their gazes met.

"We do this as equals." She winced. "I mean you're the successful business guy and I'm the college dropout—"

Javier placed a finger to her lips. "You have plenty of enthusiasm. You can, I'm quite sure, do whatever you set your mind to. Anything, Kendra, I promise. The sky's the limit."

Is this guy for real?

Then he continued, "Okay. Maybe there's a job for you at High Sierra."

Her eyes lit with pleasure. At the idea of working at a marijuana store? Well, something she hadn't tried and failed at...maybe this time she'd get it right.

Get real.

"This is ridiculous." I slashed my arm through the air.

Aaron grabbed that wayward arm and turned me toward him.

Again, his simple touch soothed. Calmed. Centered.

"I think you need to leave your sister to sort things out herself. Perhaps we can have a late lunch at my restaurant today?" Aaron glanced between Kendra, Javier, and me. "The four of us?"

Javier stood and helped Kendra to her feet. Again, he wrapped an arm around her and pulled her tight toward him.

Possessive much?

"That's very kind of you, Aaron. Kendra and I would be delighted to join you." He cast me a wary gaze. "If it's a friendly gathering amongst friends."

Aaron tightened his grip on my arm. "All friendly, I promise."

"I'll be on my best behavior." A promise I didn't want to make, but—for everyone's sake—I'd put in the effort. In truth, I didn't care what Javier thought of me—but I wanted to mend fences with Kendra.

And I wanted Aaron to respect me.

Javier offered his hand.

I didn't want to take it, but convention dictated that I do so. After an endless moment, I reciprocated.

When we finished shaking and released, Kendra planted herself in front of me and cupped my cheek. "I appreciate that you want to protect me—but I need to do this by myself. If I'm going to make a mistake, I have to do it alone."

But I didn't want her to make a mistake. As her big brother, I wanted to protect her from all the shit that could happen in the world.

Wordlessly, I nodded and stepped back from her.

Aaron guided me back toward the booths and away from the field. "I'm sorry."

"Nothing to be sorry for. It's a glorious day with a bright, shining sun. It's early enough in the morning that we aren't facing the press of crowds, and we're going to have a lovely lunch with your sister and her fiancé."

I tripped.

Aaron righted me.

I wasn't known for being clumsy, and my cheeks—which had just started to return to normal temperature—flared heat again. "God, this is so embarrassing." I met his gaze. "Sorry."

I read nothing but compassion in those dark-brown orbs.

His eyes crinkled at the side when he smiled. "All good. The ground can be uneven."

Not breaking eye contact, I opted not to look down. I knew very well that the ground was even—my equilibrium was off because my sister wanted to marry a pothead and live the hippie life in California. Heedless of what immigration authorities thought of this harebrained scheme. "Are they crazy, or am I?"

He scratched his nose. "Miriam Vincent is a crackerjack lawyer. We'll put in a call to her, and hopefully tomorrow she can meet with you and you can figure out what is possible and not possible. She doesn't specialize in immigration, but she would've studied it at law school. If she can't help, she'll recommend someone who can."

"That simple?" Things never worked out that easily for me.

"Yep. We can either bring Kendra with us, or we can fill her in after the fact."

"We?" I couldn't have heard right.

An easy shrug. "I haven't seen Miriam in a while. Unless there's confidential information you plan to exchange that you don't want me to hear." He appeared easygoing about it—as if it didn't matter either way.

Well, it did to me. You can take the time off work?"

"Of course. I'm the boss." He offered me a winning smile. His teeth were perfectly straight and very white. "I have Lynne cleaning the rooms and Jason on the desk—we're golden."

I was pretty sure—after such a busy weekend—that there'd be more to do. Still, if he was offering, I wouldn't turn down the help. "Yes, please."

"Great."

He still held my arm.

Part of me wanted to point out that I was steadier now and could stand on my own. The other part really liked how solidly he held me. I was always the one people relied on—leaning on someone solid and strong felt good.

"Now, do you want to wander through the stalls, or do you want to go back to the inn? I figure we have about an hour before Kendra and Javier come around. I'll need to secure a reservation—we're pretty busy. If not, I'm sure they wouldn't mind if I entertained them in my home."

His home was lovely, so I found no fault in his offer. In fact, a bit of privacy might be preferred. "Whatever works for you. Although I feel guilty that you're going through this much trouble."

"Nonsense. The whole point of having a place of my own is so I can entertain friends."

"You barely know me. You barely know Kendra." At least I assumed that was the case. She'd only been in town a few days.

Another casual shrug. "You and Kendra are good people—people I'd choose to be friends with. I've known Javier for most of his life."

"He's younger than you, right?" I couldn't begin to guess at Aaron's age, but he had an air about him that didn't seem nearly as young as Javier.

"I'm about twelve years older than him."

I cocked my head in contemplation.

He smiled. "He's thirty-one and I'm forty-two."

"Jesus...he's older than me?" That thought hit hard. I'd assumed Kendra'd hooked up with some young stud—her usual type. She didn't tend to go for a lot of substance with her choice of companions.

Aaron laughed. "Javier's been running his business for several years—he was one of the first to set up shop in this area—just a couple months after pot was legalized. He's got a solid five years of business acumen behind him. I haven't seen the financials, but he certainly seems to be doing well."

I'd only been in business for six years—having started my own marketing-and-consulting firm right out of business school. School I'd attended part-time while taking care of Kendra. Our mother died when my sister was fifteen and I was twenty. I dropped out of the prestigious University of British Columbia to come back to Mission City and attend the local university. I'd balanced school and trying to corral my lawless sister. Sometimes, I doubted I'd done either particularly well. Still, she hadn't been arrested, and I had a thriving business. Okay, so maybe I'd done better than I gave myself credit for.

"Those are some deep thoughts." Aaron tapped my frown line. "Why don't we head back? If you want, we can stop in at High Sierra on the way."

How had he known? That was exactly what I wanted to do. "Will Javier see us?"

"He's probably gone home to shower before lunch."

Yes, that'd be logical. And Kendra would be with him so... "Yes, I want to see the store."

Finally, Aaron let go of my arm. I didn't want him to, though. I wanted to continue to cling to him. These feelings of neediness were so alien and yet also so pervasive. I wanted whatever he could offer me. If I'd been bolder, I would've snagged his hand and held it as we walked down the street.

But I wasn't bold.

I wasn't strong like that.

We didn't know each other that way.

Oh, I'd spotted a few rainbow flags in town, so I didn't get a homophobic vibe. Still, I'd learned to be careful over the years—Mission City was getting better—but we were still in the Bible Belt of Cedar Valley. Plenty of people didn't approve of *alternative* lifestyles.

Whatever.

My business was built on being gay-friendly.

"That frown line is liable to become permanent." Aaron flashed me a grin.

I hadn't even noticed him watching me. I removed my sunglasses. "This is all new to me."

He gestured between the two of us. "Having a guy friend?"

A snicker escaped. "No, having my sister proposing to some guy I don't know, in a country that's basically foreign, and me having no say or control."

"Do you ever control Kendra?"

Damn. "Well, I try to look out for her. Our mother died when Kendra was still a teenager, and I had to take care of her. It's been a struggle to let go of that tight control and let her make her own mistakes."

"Your dad?"

"Our father left when I was young and Kendra was only a baby. He reappeared in our lives about a year ago—out of nowhere. He bought Kendra a bike. A Yamaha which she promptly traded for her Harley."

"Sweet ride."

"If you say so."

"I do."

"Oh shit. You're one of them." I wasn't sure I could put more derision in the word.

"What did your father try to buy you with?"

His change of topic—or evasion, I wasn't sure—caught me off-guard. "He, uh, offered to invest in my business. To help me grow. Basically, he waved a contract for big bucks under my nose. Nepotism at its worse. His company was looking for a new PR firm, and he was ready to sign me on without any competition. Which, I might add, went expressly against corporate policy." I sighed. "Whether he was doing it from a good place or not, we would've been breaking the rules."

"And you never knowingly break the rules."

"Pretty much."

"You turned him down."

I scratched my scalp. "Yep. Would've been the biggest contract of my career. I could've opened a proper office and hired real staff."

"Yet something tells me you don't regret your decision."

Either the man knew me well or my face gave everything away. "Pretty much. After I turned him down, I applied for the open bidding process. I didn't even make the cut—nor should I have. I didn't have the breadth of experience necessary to take on that kind of job. Hell, I might never get there."

"Is that a bad thing?"

I shook my head. "No, I'm not cut out for corporate like that. I like helping entrepreneurs and people starting out. Or people pivoting to make their businesses more inclusive. I wouldn't be able to do that if I was schilling for him."

Aaron tapped my forehead. "You did good." He indicated the store we'd stopped in front of. "Ready?"

"Sure." Truly, I was curious to find out more about this guy who just might wind up marrying my sister.

Chapter Four

Aaron

I'd only been in High Sierra twice before—once on opening day, and once when Javier'd asked me to drop off some inn brochures. At the same time, I'd snagged some of his to keep under our desk to provide to any guests who might express an interest in recreational marijuana.

After getting a nod from Noel, I held the door open for him.

Since all the product was in sealed packages, the store didn't smell like anything more than the flowers that lined the front window.

"Hey, Aaron." Griff offered me an enormous wave.

The man was taller than me, lankier than me, and way younger than me. His red hair always flopped in the most-perfect style, and his green eyes always sparkled. Okay, except when they were hazy from imbibing—but he only ever did that outside of work. Javier'd lucked out on nabbing Griff just out of college, and the young man had a strong work ethic. He also had a tendency to goof off a bit. Ah, the joys of youth.

"Who's your friend?" Griff nodded toward Noel.

"This is Noel. Kendra's older brother." I was taking a gamble that Griff'd met Kendra, and his huge smile assured me he had.

He grinned. "I would've put the moves on her, but I could see Javier was smitten. Well, kind of irritated and smitten. And protective and..." He snapped his fingers. "You're the cause of all the ruckus last night, aren't you?"

Noel winced. "Likely."

Griff waved him off. "We need more excitement in town."

I wasn't sure we did, but that was just me. I liked things to be as tranquil as the proverbial pond in summer. Griff loved a storm by the ocean.

To each his own.

Griff eyed us. "You here for some product, or are you here to check out Javier's store?"

Before either of us could answer, he continued, "Javier runs a grand establishment. Top notch. He follows all the regulations, and we've never had a problem with the authorities. He's a great boss who treats his employees fairly—he, like, gave me time off when my dad was dying. Paid time off," he was quick to add.

I cut a glance at Noel who appeared appropriately impressed. From what I'd heard, Canada had more social programs to take care of people in need. Many American companies argued giving people paid time off would hurt the bottom line. I didn't feel that way—and apparently neither did Javier. I respected him for that.

"How's Louella?" Javier's employee had recently gone into premature labor and had a healthy, although definitely early, baby.

"Oh, hang on." Griff yanked his phone out of his back pocket. He scrolled for a bit, then handed me the phone.

The most perfect little baby was on the screen. Hard to tell in the photograph, but clearly tiny. "Carmela's adorable."

Griff puffed out his chest. "Javier and I are going to be honorary uncles."

Which spoke to Javier's care of his employees—that they felt such a high level of loyalty.

"Javier's arranged paid leave and—" He clapped his hand over his mouth. "—I wasn't supposed to say anything."

I tilted my head. "He's worried pregnant women will flock to work here?"

Griff smiled wryly. "Uh, that hadn't been what I was thinking. Not at all. Just…some businesses might not appreciate looking stingy with their maternity leave policy."

Ah. Well, I had a generous one as well, but also didn't advertise that fact. I hesitated. *Go for it.* "I think Javier and Kendra just got engaged."

Noel shot me an indecipherable look. Not quite a glare. Not quite a question. Definitely not happy, though.

Griff clapped his hands in glee. His smile was broad. "Oh, I'm going to close the store for a few minutes at lunch and run out to get streamers and champagne. This is the best news ever. I mean, I love Javier—and so do the women—but I despaired of him ever finding *the one.*"

"So he's gone through a lot of women?"

That appeared to trip up Griff, and he visibly stuttered at Noel's question—opening his mouth once or twice like a landed fish. Finally, he held up his index finger. "Is there a right way to answer that?"

"The truth would be nice." Noel still looked displeased.

Griff bit his lower lip. "He's seen a few women over the years—but no one seriously. He's not a player, though."

Noel didn't look convinced.

"You guys want some product? I'm sure Javier'd let you have it for free. Well, I mean he has to pay for it to account for the drop in inventory, but I'm sure, for his new brother-in-law—"

A hand went up to stop him midstream.

Noel appeared a little green. Definitely paler than his already pale skin. Guy obviously didn't spend a lot of time in the sun—or he wore SPF 60.

After a moment, though, he cocked his head and looked toward me. "Sorry, I shouldn't be speaking for you. You might—"

"I do not." Clear and concise. He didn't need to know the reason for my sobriety. I never took mood-altering substances. Not after the way I was raised.

He snagged my hand. "We might as well go. Javier and Kendra might be there shortly."

"Eh?" Griff's brow furrowed.

"Family meeting," I clarified. "Meet the future in-law."

Noel squeezed my hand tighter.

I held in the smile—but it was a near thing.

We exited High Sierra together into the cloudless day.

Noel put his sunglasses back on.

I hadn't worn mine. Maybe should have, but bright light didn't bother me. Of course, we had sunshine most of the time in California, while I knew British Columbia had a lot of rain. That being said, I'd never seen Kendra wear shades.

What does it matter?

It didn't, of course, but I wanted to know more about Noel—what made him tick, what made him smile, and, most importantly, what made him cry. I didn't want to trigger him in any way. Which was, I was quite certain, an odd quirk. Except I'd spent years trying to not set off my mother's tears, and that'd worn me down. Tiptoeing was the best way to deal with her, but it hadn't been a life.

In the end, it hadn't mattered.

I pushed that thought aside. I didn't need to think of my mother or her tragic death. For all his anger, Noel seemed like a pretty level-headed guy.

Or so you think.

More than most people, I knew looks could be deceiving.

I shook my head. All this because of sunglasses? Sometimes my mind was a scary place to be.

Still, Noel held my hand as we silently returned to the inn. When Jason'd told me that the guy he presumed was my guest had headed to the festival, I'd gotten an odd feeling in the pit of my stomach. I didn't rely on gut instinct often—I was a spreadsheet-and-numbers kind of guy—but I suspected nothing good was going to come of Noel going down there. Knowing also of the traditional flag-football game, I chose that direction.

I was damn glad I had.

When we arrived at the inn, Noel dropped my hand.

Feeling oddly bereft, I opened the door and held it open for him.

As always, the smell of food wafted into the lobby to greet us. Adding the fine dining had been a genius move, if I may say so myself. Having those mouthwatering smells warmed people as they checked in, and had them heading to the restaurant to check out the fare. My prices weren't that high—the fine dining came from the experience and not an exorbitant price tag.

"Do you mind waiting for just a moment?"

Noel shook his head and pointed to the sitting room.

I nodded.

He headed that way while I headed for the office.

"You found your friend."

Jason's baritone voice warmed me. He'd come aboard with me not long after I bought the place using an inheritance. I'd offered him a management role, but he preferred working with guests. He was as integral to this operation as I was—or perhaps even more so.

"I did, thanks. He's in the sitting room for a few minutes while I check on the progress of the room cleaning."

He waved me off. "Lynne's all done. And I had two unexpected bookings, so we're full up again for another couple of days."

Was that a *crap* or a *hell, yes!* My new friend still needed a place to stay—unless he planned to head back to Canada soon. With things as unstable as they were with Kendra, I didn't see him hitting the road again anytime soon. Except maybe he needed to go back as soon as possible. I still didn't have a firm grasp on what he did.

Jason tilted his head. "Is that okay?"

Damn. "Of course it's okay. We're at our best when we're at capacity. Keeps us on our toes."

We did okay during the rainy season when we were slower as well, though. Gave us a chance to regroup, make upgrades, and do general maintenance. Keeping a building this old running in tiptop shape was a challenge—one I relished every day.

In the back room, I did a quick survey—found everything in perfect order—and headed back into the lobby and over to the sitting room. A few guests lounged in chairs. Some read, some scrolled on their phone, and one sat at the mahogany antique desk and worked away industriously at their laptop. All the rooms had small desks and strong Wi-Fi, but some guests preferred being amongst other people—even as they did a solitary pursuit.

Noel stood by the bookcase. We carried a variety of reading material—from the classics to modern-day stuff. Guests were free to take a book and leave a book—except the classic sets, of course. Noel ran his hand along one of the spines.

I joined him and took a look. *Moby Dick*. Well, okay then. "Have you read the book?"

He shook his head. "My school favored Canadian literature. I can tell you all about *The Stone Angel* by Margaret Laurence, but I know almost nothing about American literature. The English Department had a broad range of courses at my university, but I stuck to professional writing."

"Ah, do you write manuals and stuff? Are you any good at computers?"

A guffaw escaped. "I'm in marketing—I run my own public-relations firm. I studied English grammar and stuff. Then took business courses. A few accounting ones as well."

I smiled. "I should get you to look over the inn's marketing and promotion material—hasn't had a makeover in about five years."

"I'm sure it's fine." He bit his lower lip. "But I can look it over if you'd like. I feel like I owe you more than advice on brochures."

"See, it's not that way at all." I brushed my hand along his arm. "You don't owe me anything. I'm just helping out a new friend. And her brother," I added.

His mouth twitched. "I should at least rent a room."

"Sorry, no can do. The inn is full—literally. I don't have a single spare room."

"And no manger I can sleep in?"

I loved this teasing side of Noel—and wished I saw more of it. Oh well, I'd have to work harder to bring it out.

"No mangers to be found. And you're not sleeping in your car." I grinned. "So you'll just have to settle for the sofa bed. Or the actual bed...if you dare."

He tilted his head. "Dare?"

"I'll explain later."

As he grabbed my hand, I stopped.

Our gazes clashed.

His pupils dilated.

Ah, so not ignorant. I felt something between the two of us—a deep and abiding need to claim. Or be claimed. I was easy and could happily go either way.

This is nuts. You've known him a day.

True...but I'd never felt for anyone else what I felt for him. More than sexual attraction—although that was there, for sure. But something deeper. More enduring.

Folly.

He was Canadian. I was American. We both had busy lives more than a thousand miles apart.

Kendra and Javier are making it work.

Yeah, but they were young and naïve. They didn't have the experience I possessed, and that I suspected Noel did as well.

Still, our gazes held. His eyes blazed blue fire.

"Tonight we need to talk."

As much as I'd prefer to do other things, talking worked.

After a quick glance around the room to ensure no one noticed, I pecked his cheek. Then I withdrew and indicated we should go back to the lobby and, obviously, on to the restaurant.

A long moment passed before he broke eye contact and headed out.

I'm in for a world of hurt.

And I don't even care.

I'd deal with the pain tomorrow. Today, I wanted the pleasure.

Chapter Five

Noel

Aaron had a hand firmly at my back when we approached the maître d' station.

A lovely younger woman with fiery red curls wore a smart suit of navy trousers, a white blouse, and a navy jacket.

"Hello, Jeanette."

She offered a wide smile. "Hello back. Come to check us out?"

He chuckled. "No. I know you're doing a spectacular job. Lots of online reviews with raves."

I made a note to look them up and add one of my own. I might omit mentioning the fact I was staying in the owner's suite...

"The table you requested is set up."

"Great, thank you." Aaron took four menus from her. "Javier and his fiancée, Kendra, will be here shortly. Can you bring them through?"

Jeanette's green eyes lit. "Oh, that's exciting. I hadn't heard about that."

"Recent development."

She nodded. "Fair enough. Kat is your server. They'll take great care of you."

They? So...non-binary? Didn't matter to me except that I needed to be careful when using their pronoun. I spent a lot of time educating my clients about inclusive language. Some picked it up right away—others struggled.

Aaron guided me through the restaurant and out to the back deck.

I put my sunglasses back on. Might be rude, but I was sensitive to light and so tended to keep them handy.

He offered me the seat in the shade, which I gladly accepted while he took the seat next to me after he placed the menus on the table.

Glancing at it quickly, I tried to determine what my stomach could and couldn't tolerate. I was a guy who could eat almost anything—except when my stomach was in knots. Which, admittedly, didn't happen often. Actually, pretty much only Kendra could upset me. I was surprised I hadn't developed an ulcer with all the worrying I did about her.

Speak of the devil.

I spotted Kendra and Javier wending their way through the tables.

As Aaron had with me, Javier's arm was firmly at Kendra's back.

I tried not to stiffen as I rose.

Aaron did as well.

Javier offered his hand to me and I shook it.

See? I can be an adult.

And he was older than me, for Christ's sake. He didn't look it, though. Not a baby face, but no lines of maturity either. He held out Kendra's chair, and she sat.

Within moments, an androgynous-looking person approached our table with a huge smile. "Hi, boss."

Aaron smiled. "Hello Kat. You know Javier."

They nodded.

"This is his fiancée, Kendra, and Kendra's brother, Noel."

If Kat noticed Aaron's hand on the back of my chair, they didn't comment. "What can I get everyone to drink?"

"A bottle of champagne with three glasses. And ice water."

They nodded and headed off.

"Really, we don't need champagne." Javier scratched his shaved head.

Aaron waved him off. "This is a celebration—have whatever you'd like. My treat."

Both Javier and I started to argue, but Aaron held up his hand—forestalling us.

"I don't have friends over nearly as often as I should. This was my idea, this is my restaurant, therefore, this is my treat."

Javier caught my eye. Yeah, he wasn't thrilled either. Still, I couldn't argue with Aaron's logic—except I wasn't paying him for a room either. I needed to find a way to contribute more than I was.

Kendra bounced in her seat like a two-year-old. Endearing and annoying at the same time. But that was so Kendra.

I picked up the menu. The prices were less than I expected of such an establishment—except people wore clothes of every kind. From daytime formal to shorts and ratty T-shirt casual. Still, the ambiance spoke of elegance and expense. Aaron'd figured out how to hit just the right note so everyone felt welcome here, but the experience was still a special one. I'd have to ask him how he'd done it.

"The blackened chicken fettuccini Alfredo sounds delicious." Kendra toyed with a lock of her long hair. "Although that might be a bit heavy."

"They make the best burgers in town," Javier said, putting down his menu. Then he looked around as if worried he'd get caught. "But The Copper Moon comes a close second."

The Copper... Oh, right, I'd spotted the restaurant during my walk earlier today. Maybe I could take Aaron there—my treat.

"What are you thinking, Noel?"

Aaron's question pulled me from my introspection.

"Uh, whatever you think."

Kendra cocked her head.

I rubbed my face, noting the stubble, and wishing I'd shaved. I always looked better when I shaved. "I'm easy." Truthfully, I didn't want to have to make a decision. I still sought the right words to say to my sister about making one of the biggest mistakes of her life.

Aaron tilted his head, much as Kendra had.

Sheesh.

"The steak is divine. You okay with salad? We offer fries..."

"Steak and salad is perfect." Whatever. I didn't care.

"And a baked potato," Kendra added. "He loves baked potatoes."

I blinked. She was right. She was absolutely right. I'd just had no notion that she knew that about me. I wasn't sure she knew anything about me. With five years between us, we'd never been close. I'd certainly watched out for her. When she was a toddler because our mother wasn't coping well. As a young adult because our mother had cancer. Then as a teenager because we'd been essentially orphans. I knew way too much about her life.

Or at least I thought I did.

I knew about the jobs, the guys, the heartbreaks, and the vindications. In my heart, I believed I knew my sister. The woman sitting before me? Poised and collected. Excited, for sure, but calm. Calmer than I ever remembered seeing her. When she was younger, I'd tried to see if she had some kind of attention or hyperactivity problem, but no one'd been willing to diagnose her. Now, as she flourished, I was glad she didn't have that label hanging over her.

While she held Javier's hand, she reached out to touch my arm with the other.

Our gazes met.

"I pay attention, Noel. I know it doesn't always feel that way, but I do. I know what you've sacrificed to get me here—"

I waved my other hand.

She glared. "I know. I've always known. And I haven't been grateful enough—that's on me. I promise I'll be more gracious in the future. Plus…" Her face lit, and she glanced toward Javier before looking back. "I won't be coming back to your basement. You can ship my stuff down here and get your life back."

Goddammit.

Had I really made her feel like she was that much of a burden to me? Admittedly, I had days when the weight of the world was crushing me, and she usually centered in whatever chaos I faced. "I love you."

Great, just blurt it out.

Her blue eyes shimmered, and she blinked several times.

"You've never been a burden. You're my sister. I'd do anything for you. I just want you happy."

She squeezed my hand. "Javier makes me happy, Noel. Really, really, really happy. Like nothing I've ever felt. And I care about him so much. I want to be my best self for him."

"Hey." Javier frowned. "I love you just the way you are."

Her face softened, and she blinked again.

Aaron cleared his throat.

We all turned to him.

"I think we're in agreement that we want Kendra happy, Kendra is happy with Javier, and they need to make their own decisions as to how to best live their lives."

Well, nailed it in one.

"Uh, yeah, I guess so."

Javier met my gaze. "I'll do everything in my power to take care of her. To see that her every need is met."

Kendra scowled. "You don't need to talk about me like I'm not here. I'm a grown woman who's perfectly capable of caring for herself."

Inwardly I winced. I held my tongue. A series of poor decisions had led to her taking a break. Those troubles she'd left behind were still there—apparently messes I'd need to take care of since she didn't even seem to be aware of them.

Huh.

Maybe her staying in California was a good thing—for one last time, I could clean up her mess, and she could have a fresh start.

Hope Javier knows what he's getting himself into.

Kat approached the table, notepad at the ready.

I sat back—metaphorically—and let everyone else order. Including letting Aaron order for me. Admittedly, this was completely out of character for me. But, somehow, letting someone else take control just this once felt good. I felt like maybe, just maybe, everything might work out.

Small talk ensued, and although I followed the conversation, I didn't contribute much.

When Kat had removed the plates and we'd all declined dessert, Kendra rose.

"I need to, you know..."

"Past the bar and on your right." Aaron's smooth direction.

"Thanks."

All three of us had risen with her and, as she disappeared back inside, Aaron and I sat.

Javier remained standing. After a long moment, he pulled his phone out of his back pocket. "May I have your father's phone number?"

"What?" I mustn't have heard him correctly.

"It's only proper that I ask for your sister's hand."

I shifted, but Aaron placed a hand on my arm.

"Javier's a traditionalist."

Perhaps Aaron sensed my disquiet. Our father'd had nothing to do with Kendra for most of her twenty-three years. He'd only reappeared in the last year and was ingratiating himself with gifts. Ones Kendra embraced, like the bike—and ones I rejected flatly, like the contract to work for his company.

Part of me railed against this. If this young man was to ask anyone for Kendra's hand in marriage—and this truly was too archaic to contemplate—it should be me.

"Give him your dad's number."

I turned to meet Aaron's gaze. After a long moment, I pulled out my phone, scrolled to my father's contact information, and read the number off to Javier.

He typed it into his phone and then, after a quick nod, headed back into the restaurant.

"Where's he going?"

"Either to the sitting room or to the street, I would guess." Aaron offered a smile. "We'll cover for him when Kendra gets back."

"Oh, we will, will we?" I didn't like duplicity. Still, Aaron had a point. If our father refused, or if he wanted to extract some kind of promise from Javier, the man was better off on his own.

Before I could form another thought, Kendra breezed back.

Aaron and I rose.

She looked at Javier's empty seat. Then looked at me. And glared.

I held up my hands. "He needed to step away. He'll be back. I promise."

Technically I didn't have the right to make the promise, but whatever. If Javier didn't come back, then that said more about him than anything I ever could. Maybe, if he didn't come back, I could convince Kendra her affections were misplaced.

On cue, Javier returned. His phone was in his back pocket, and he showed no outward sign of what'd happened.

I was dying to ask—but I wouldn't.

He pressed a kiss to Kendra's cheek before resuming his seat and grasping her hand.

"Everything okay?"

"Everything's perfect, my love. Everything's perfect." He met my gaze, and I read the warning. Or the promise.

Whatever.

He'd tell her in his own time, I guessed.

And our father might call her to congratulate her. Or he might call me to yell that I wasn't doing a good enough job of caring for her. I figured each option had about a fifty-fifty chance.

I'd barely known my father when he'd abandoned us when I was seven, and I hadn't let him in when he'd returned. Maybe that was wrong of me. But the sense of loss when he'd walked out the door had been profound—most especially because I had to watch my beloved mother suffer so much.

"Noel?"

I snapped my gaze up to meet Aaron's, who beckoned to me.

"Kendra and Javier are leaving."

In fact, the two were already standing.

I rose as well. I kissed Kendra on the cheek and shook Javier's hand. After a moment, they left.

Before I could sit back down, Aaron grabbed my arm. "Why don't we head up to my place? We can talk. Privately."

In that moment, I considered that the entire afternoon hadn't been private—and events would impact not just Aaron and Javier, as residents of this town, but Kendra now as well.

"Yeah, private." I let him guide me away even as I pondered what my life would be like without always having to clean up my sister's messes.

Or, if Javier was going to be the biggest mistake of all.

Chapter Six

Aaron

Taking Noel back to my room wasn't strictly necessary—but the guy was flummoxed, with a permanent v in his forehead. If he didn't get things off his chest, he was liable to explode.

Well, I wasn't positive about that—but pretty damn close.

My employees had things well in hand, as they always did, and we headed upstairs. I swiped my card. As he entered the room, a thought occurred. "I need to get you a swipe card." I closed the door, dropping my keyring and my wallet with the swipe card on the table strategically placed at the front door for just this purpose.

"I..." He scratched his scalp. "Am I staying that long?"

I moved to the junk drawer—something I'd sworn I'd never have—pulled out the second card, and handed it to him.

Without much thought—or at least that was my perception—he pulled out his wallet, tucked away the card, and put it back into his back pocket. Then he pulled it out again, along with his cell phone, and put them on the dining room table.

I'd reminded him to charge the phone last night, so I didn't worry about it needing to be hooked up to a charger now.

Then, like a balloon deflating after a pinprick, he dropped to the couch. He'd put it back to rights—which I appreciated—and he'd neatly stacked the blanket, sheet, and pillow on my bed.

A weird feeling had pervaded me when I'd spotted them when I'd come up to see if he was awake. I'd headed back downstairs to have Jason direct me to the festival. Thank God he had. Likely Javier and Noel wouldn't have come to blows.

Or so I hoped.

But the thought of a man having stepped into my inner sanctuary? That didn't happen often.

Okay, like ever.

I was a proud gay man. In a community that was LGBTQ-friendly. But I still did very little dating.

Okay, like never.

And why was that? In this moment, I struggled for a reason. I told myself all the standard ones—I hadn't met the right man. Enforced celibacy could be a good thing. I didn't have sexual desire toward anyone. I didn't think I was ACE—asexual—but it'd been a damn long time since I'd looked at a guy and thought *yeah, I want to bring him home and get sweaty in the sheets with him.*

Oh, and my grandmother wouldn't approve.

Well, again, I couldn't state that for a fact. I'd never come out. She'd never asked. She hadn't pressed me about finding a *nice girl* to settle down with either.

You're overthinking—

"Hey, what is going on in that mind of yours?"

I glanced down at Noel who had a frown on his face. "I thought I was deep into contemplation. But you? Like you're on another planet. Or your mind is far away."

"Possibly both?"

"Are you thinking I didn't do the right thing? That I should've taken a harder line? Or that I should've been more lenient?"

Of course, I hadn't been thinking either of those things.

I pointed to the couch.

He frowned. Then, as if understanding dawned, he patted the seat beside him.

"Oh. Do you want water? I also have lemonade, iced tea—"

"Do you have vodka I can add to it?"

"Uh..."

"Shit. Right, you don't drink. And I don't need it." He rushed on. "In fact, I hardly ever drink. And I don't want to say that Kendra's pushed me close a few times—even though she has. I'm more of a celebration drinker when I land a contract or something goes really well. And I always go out with friends—I never drink alone."

How does he know? Solo drinking was a huge trigger for me. My dad used to come home from work and drink almost to the point of oblivion.

Almost.

But never so far gone as to not—

Don't go there.

Noel rose. "I love lemonade and don't drink it nearly as often as I'd like. Sugar, you know?"

I did know. Therefore, the stuff was a treat for me as well.

We moved to the kitchen together. The space consisted of a counter, a fridge, a dishwasher, and a sink against part of the back wall of the large, airy apartment. Truthfully, I didn't spend much time cooking. With amazing food at my fingertips—and needing to do quality control, of course—I tended to eat out a lot. I was careful with portion control because I really didn't want to have a paunch or get diabetes—both things that happened regularly in the males of my family. I enjoyed brisk walks in the early morning along the Rio Luminita. Fresh dew on the morning grass. Sometimes mist coming off the water. Just a soothing time to listen to an audiobook and let the world go past.

After pulling the jug of lemonade out of the fridge, I snagged two glasses.

Noel stood near the end of the counter, by the microwave, and leaned so his hip hit the counter. Completely relaxed in my space. Perhaps less stressed about his sister?

I liked that idea. Well, both ideas. I wanted him comfortable here, and I wanted him to fret less about his sister. After I poured the glass, I handed it to him.

He took it gratefully, offering a wide smile. After a sip, he sighed. "I really needed that."

"You deserved that."

He cocked his head.

"I appreciate how mature you were over lunch." I indicated we should head back to the couch. "That couldn't have been easy for you. I know I'd lose my mind if my brother came and told me he's getting married."

"How old is your brother?"

"Twenty-two."

"So, Kendra's age."

"Yeah."

"You understand my panic."

I shrugged. "Well, they say boys mature more slowly than girls."

Noel frowned.

Yeah, okay, that wouldn't apply to him. He'd been guardian to his sister after their mother died. And had watched out for her before, if I understood correctly. He'd had to grow up quickly.

"Trey has been in college for the past four years. He's lived a pretty sheltered life. That's not to say he hasn't had problems—just that they're not adult-world problems."

"You paid for his education."

Said with absolute certainty.

He wasn't wrong.

"My mother died, leaving me a large estate. Trey wasn't her son, so he didn't get anything. Our father was useless, and his mother...had problems."

Noel's eyebrow quirked, but I wasn't going there.

"Anyway... What I'm trying to say is that it appears Kendra's got some real-world experience. That's valuable."

"She's failed at a bunch of stuff."

We sat.

I angled myself so I faced him, tucking one leg under my butt. Wasn't the most comfortable position, but it'd do.

If I reached out my arm, I could flutter my hand across his stubbly brush cut.

My own hair was just about as short. Sometimes I let it grow out, but it had a tendency to curl in weird ways. Keeping it short negated those awkward tendencies.

"Failed at what stuff? Life is full of ups and downs."

"The missteps are too numerous to count. Don't get me wrong, I love her. I know I keep saying that—"

"But sometimes you have to remind yourself?"

"This last mess...the guy she was working for sued her."

I cocked my head.

He waved his hand. "She doesn't know, and I've cleaned up the mess, so please don't tell her." He scratched his scalp. "I mean, I should probably tell her so she can, I don't know, learn some lesson. But I don't think she will, and..." He waved his hand around ineffectually.

I snagged his hand and lowered it to his thigh. *I should withdraw.* But I wasn't going to. My hand now rested on his thigh and I had no intention of moving it until he asked.

"How bad was the mess?"

"I fixed the lawsuit—and it didn't cost all that much money. I had to do some serious groveling, though, and that hurt."

Likely his pride. "Does anyone know?"

"Nah. I'll give the guy props. He saw humiliating me in public would likely garner sympathy—me being the innocent party—and sentiment might turn against him. So I did what I had to do."

"Could you ask your father to help?"

His entire body shuddered. "Uh, no. Regardless of what you think a father/son relationship should be...well, we don't have it. Him leaving when I was seven and not coming back into my life until I was twenty-seven has had a profound impact. And I'm sure I should go for some therapy or shit to work out my unresolved issues of abandonment—" He cleared his throat. "I just don't see the point. I'm not letting him back into my life in any meaningful way because I don't trust him. I've tried to warn Kendra, but she's a grown woman. As you've pointed out on numerous occasions. She's got to forge her own relationship with him."

"Maybe he's changed."

He caught and held my gaze. "Not likely. I don't get his endgame. We weren't worth having a relationship for all those years. Even when my mother died, he didn't come back. Now, suddenly, he wants us to be a cozy family? That doesn't fly with me." He blinked. "Sounds like you didn't have a good relationship with your father either."

Damn.

"I didn't. He was..." I took a sip from my lemonade and then put it on the coffee table on a coaster. I still gripped Noel's hand. After a moment, I resettled. "A vicious alcoholic. I mean, he was abusive when he wasn't drinking, don't get me wrong. But when he was into a bottle?" I rubbed my hand across my face. "I don't know why my mother stayed. Honest to God, I don't know. She came from money. Even if she faced embarrassment for having endured the violence, she could've left."

"Sometimes it's not that simple."

"He did some serious damage—to both of us. I was never so relieved as when he left. My heart broke to discover he'd married another woman because he'd gotten her pregnant. My brother was born into that situation. He's never spoken about what happened in that house—and he was only eight when our father died. I was twenty-eight and had never forgiven the man. I tried to keep an eye out for my brother, but our father made it difficult for me to see Trey. If violence went on in that household, I never knew."

Noel squeezed my hand. "I had it pretty good. Our father was never abusive, and our mother, when she sort-of recovered from his abandonment, did a decent job of raising us."

"It's not a competition." And I had the distinct impression he wasn't telling me everything. He'd implied he'd been looking out for his sister since their father left—he would've been all of seven years old. That was a hell of a responsibility for a kid. Did he ever let loose? Just have fun?

"I know it's not. I'm not even sure why I opened up, except..." His blue eyes were somber. "Except I think we both had things we needed to get off our chests."

He wasn't wrong.

"True. We're getting to know each other."

For a long moment, he just held my gaze. "I like you. I like you a lot. I want to get to know you better, even knowing I'm leaving in a day or two."

Well, that was honest. "I'm a big believer in seizing the day—that tomorrow isn't promised."

"So if I asked to kiss you?"

I swallowed. Hard. "I'd give enthusiastic consent."

He put his drink on the coffee table and scooted closer.

I met him halfway.

He took my cheeks in his hands—one warm from where it'd held mine and one cold from where he'd held his glass.

Our gazes locked...

My eyes drifted shut as we pressed our lips together. Lightly, at first. Just a touch. Just an exploration.

I grasped his biceps for support.

He stroked my cheekbones with his thumbs. Then he nipped at my lower lip.

Surprised, I opened my mouth.

He slid his tongue inside.

Languid. Just plain slow and sweet. I tasted the lemonade and something intangible. His scent invaded my senses—something sort of woodsy, which was a little incongruous.

Finally, he pulled back. And pressed his forehead to mine. "Thank you."

I chuckled. "Not sure I did much."

"Well, it's been a little while for me."

I considered asking how long, but then I'd have to admit my semi-permanent dry spell, and that was somewhere I didn't want to go in this moment. My cock had perked up a bit—but only a bit. I thought I wanted more, and yet I was also perfectly satisfied.

"Do you want to watch a movie or something?" I indicated my television.

"Frankly, I'd just like to cuddle."

Without words, was the unspoken part of the request.

I sat back and pulled him toward me. To my shock, he laid his head in my lap, facing the blank screen. With one hand, I lazily stroked his scalp—occasionally using my blunt fingernails to elicit a moan from him. My other hand gripped his arm. Anchoring him to me. Ensuring he knew he was safe.

We stayed that way for a very long time.

And I didn't want this to end.

Chapter Seven

Noel

S afe. I couldn't remember ever having felt so safe. I drifted off at one point, only waking when my bladder began to make demands. I sat up slowly, surprised to find a knitted blanket covering me.

Aaron met my gaze as I smiled sheepishly. Then he stroked my cheek. "You needed that."

"Yeah, I guess I did. It's been a pretty crazy few days." I indicated the bathroom, and he nodded. I pissed and tried to make myself look presentable. Shave? Nah, too much effort. And Aaron might think I was trying too hard. Which I was, in a way. Something about the man intrigued me and I wanted to get to know him better.

Shouldn't you be, you know, heading back to Canada?

I shushed my inner critic. I hadn't taken a day's vacation in—

Huh.

Well, probably I wasn't allowed to count the time I had an acute case of strep. Or the time my car broke down and I was stranded in

Quesnel for two days. I'd sworn that was the last time I visited a client in person who lived that far north. Nope, if they weren't within a couple of hours, and felt they needed personal service, I gently passed on their contract—no matter how much money it was worth.

I shook my head. Okay, so I was due for a vacation. I had my laptop because, of course I did. I could shoot off emails to my two part-time employees and let them know I'd be out of touch for a few days. Good chance Aaron had Wi-Fi in here, so I could check periodically and deal with any crises. But, dammit, I deserved a few days off. Maybe stay the week and head back Friday?

If he wants you to stay.

Well, valid point. He hadn't actually extended the invitation. He might get tired of me crashing on his couch. Although, surely a room would open up now the festival was over.

Deciding to play it by ear—but also be wary of wearing out my welcome—I stepped from the bathroom.

He stood nearby. As we passed, he snagged me around the waist and pressed a kiss to my cheek. "I enjoy having you here."

Then he was gone—disappearing into the bathroom.

My cheek tingled.

Something about this man—something indefinable to me. I loved his kisses—all gentle and sweet and then a little hot with a touch of demanding. But we hadn't done anything past kissing. Which was fine, because I never had an expectation of more. I wouldn't have minded if he'd made more moves on me, though.

You're just lonely.

Better than horny.

Well, okay, then.

And I wasn't feeling an overwhelming physical desire. Just a nice slow and steadily growing attraction. I liked the way his mind worked.

I appreciated how he'd grown up in shitty circumstances but had done well for himself. Not everyone would've come out of it doing so well. That being said, he'd had a younger sibling counting on him. I was aware how powerful that could be.

I moved to the living room, scooped up the two abandoned glasses of lemonade, and took them to the kitchen. Shame to waste them, but they were warm now. I poured them down the drain and placed the glasses in the dishwasher.

Aaron came up to me from behind and pressed himself against me. He wrapped his arms around my chest and nuzzled my neck. "How long can you stay?"

"A few days." Said on an exhalation.

"I'll take it."

"Shouldn't I, you know, get a room?"

He pressed closer. He wasn't erect, but my cock stirred at his nearness. "Only if you want to. I'm very happy having you here with me."

"Then I'll stay." Simple decision. Would also keep me close to Kendra if things went sideways.

After a moment, he laid his cheek against my shoulder blade—an oddly endearing gesture.

I blinked several times. This position we were in...was more intimate than any of my paltry hookups over the past few years. I hadn't been looking for more, and the guys hadn't been interested. I kept telling myself that once the business was successful, then I could look at finding a partner. Except, to be brutally honest, my business—by every possible metric—was successful. I'd been profitable since the end of the first year. My home was mostly paid off. I had a couple of part-time employees whom I paid well. I could pick and choose my clients—although I pretty much took everyone who was genuinely interested in becoming more inclusive.

"What're you thinking?" Aaron's breath skittered across the back of my neck.

I shivered, and it had nothing to do with being cold. "Just wondering if it's time for dinner—I'm starving."

He chuckled. Did he know I was only half-serious? That I wanted more, but wasn't sure how to ask for it?

Finally, after a long moment, he pulled back. Gently, he turned me in his arms. "Why don't we head to The Copper Moon?"

"Sure." Sounded like a safe place to hang out. And we might run into Kendra and Javier. Well, probably not."

Aaron tapped my forehead. "We'll see them tomorrow, I'm sure."

My phone buzzed on the table. I broke away from Aaron to head over and pick it up. "Oh, a text from Miriam Vincent. She says she can see me at nine tomorrow morning." I'd hoped the lawyer could fit me in early in the week, but first thing Monday morning was better service than I could've expected.

"Great. We can have breakfast and head right over." Aaron stood just a few inches from me, having approached quietly.

I turned to him. "You don't have to come—I'm certain you've got plenty of stuff to do. You've already dedicated a lot of time to me."

He tilted his head. "Do you not want me to come? Because it's totally fine—"

Moving swiftly, I pressed my finger to his lips. "Of course I want you to come. I need to be up early to send a few emails, but then my decks'll be cleared and I can focus on Kendra and her needs."

Aaron puckered his lips and kissed my finger.

I withdrew it.

He smiled. "I just think you could use a friend."

Instead of feeling miffed he was only offering friendship, I returned his smile. I sensed the friends thing was the floor of this relationship—not the ceiling.

My stomach rumbled.

"Yeah, me too." Aaron snagged my hand. "Let's go."

We headed out of the inn and down the street.

The sun was setting to the west with beautiful streaks of pink and purple.

I also spotted a few puffy clouds. "Does it rain here?"

He laughed. "Yes, we get some rain. But California's in a drought, so it's never really enough."

"Ah."

"And you guys?"

"We've had a couple of scorching summers with less rain than we needed, but we make up for it during the winter. Or we usually do." I remembered one summer that had lasted well into fall and the rains were late in coming—not good for the farmers. "I enjoy having a good balance of rain and sun."

"Isn't your rainy season like nine months?"

I glanced over to see his impish grin. God, he was so handsome. "Uh, not quite. But yes, we're called the wet coast for a reason."

"You know, I've never been skiing." Another gleam in his eye.

"Well, you'll just have to come up during the winter. We have a couple of small mountains near where I live and a few ski hills within a short drive. Time it right, though, and we could go up to Whistler Mountain. That's spectacular skiing. And the village in winter? Magical." God, I sounded like a tourist brochure.

"Time it right?"

"Well, it's busy all the time—but between Christmas and New Year's, it's insane."

"Christmas is also one of our busiest times of year. Guess I'll have to come visit you in January."

Said casually, as if no big deal. As if it didn't mean anything.

But it meant everything.

Again, was he being serious or facetious? Would he really turn up at my doorstep? Because, Christ knew, I wanted him to. Just the thought of showing him my home—and my neck of the woods—held great appeal.

He met my gaze, and the little lines around his eyes crinkled. "We're here."

"You'll always be welcome."

After a moment, he nodded, his expression serious. "Same goes."

Which was nuts because we'd barely known each other twenty-four hours...and yet I just knew—deep in my soul—that I could fall for this man.

A lovely older woman greeted us at the door with a massive smile and June-bug-green glasses.

"Hello, Judy." Aaron leaned over and gave her a peck on the cheek.

She blushed. "Good to see you, Aaron." She pivoted to me. "Hello, and welcome to The Copper Moon."

"Thank you. I'm excited to be here."

"Great." She grabbed two menus. "Preference in seating?"

Aaron glanced outside. He turned to me. "Is the sun too bright? You didn't bring your sunglasses."

Something inside me lit with pleasure. He'd noticed my light sensitivity. Wow. I glanced outside. "The sun's far enough down that I'll be okay."

He turned to Judy. "A table on the patio would be lovely."

"Perfect." She led us back outside and to the only available table.

Aaron held out the chair that faced away from the sun.

I offered a genuine smile and sat.

Judy fluttered her hand after putting down the menus. "Paul will be out shortly. Water? Anything else?"

"Water's great." This time, I offered the answer. Only as Judy departed, did it occur to me Aaron might want iced tea or something. "Uh—"

He waved me off. "I was only going to have water as well. They make great shakes, but I'm interested in the grilled chicken salad."

I considered. "That sounds eerily healthy."

A guffaw escaped him. "That would be because it is."

"Ah." I gazed at the menu. "I'm having the chili with cheese and bacon." I scanned farther. "Oh, with a side of pierogies. Want to share?"

"Sure."

His smile was warm, and the flame inside me continued to burn bright. I couldn't put my finger on what about this guy attracted me so much—aside from his looks. His sincerity? His kindness? The way he treated everyone as equals?

The way his eyes sparkle when he looks at you?

Definite possibility.

"Here you go, gentlemen." A younger man with shaggy blond hair and blue eyes placed our water glasses on the table. "Are you ready to order?"

I eyed him. "Were you at the football game?" Something about him struck me as familiar.

He snapped his fingers. "Yeah, you're Kendra's older brother."

Wincing inwardly, I appreciated this might not've been the best line of questioning.

Yet he continued. "Kendra's great. And wow, her proposing to Javier? That'll be a story to tell their kids."

My stomach somersaulted. Oh, my God, they'd have kids. My irresponsible kid sister could be a mother soon.

Jesus.

Aaron rested his warm hand on my cold one. He spoke to the young man and ordered our food.

None of his words registered. Kendra marrying some guy in the abstract was one thing. My disorganized, flighty, hectic sister producing offspring was something else entirely.

"Noel?"

I glanced up.

"It's going to be okay. Your sister's going to be fine. Javier's great with kids, and I think he's always wanted one of his own. Well, maybe two, given he was an only child. And the greater Cataluma community will ensure the baby—or babies—will be well cared for. Normally I'd say the grandmother would help but..." He winced. "Millie Fernandez hasn't been the most reliable person lately. Still, I'm sure she'll be a doting grandmother."

"My father's going to be a grandfather." I couldn't think of anyone less suited for the role.

"And you're going to be an uncle."

"From a thousand miles away."

He squeezed my hand. "You can still be a force for good. And you'll just have to plan plenty of trips down here. But look, Noel, this is likely way in the future. Javier's level-headed enough to get married first before contemplating starting a family."

That thought offered mild comfort.

Well, a smidgen.

I returned the squeeze, enjoying the warmth seeping from him to me. "You swear everything's going to be okay?"

He tilted his head. "I can't make you that promise, and you wouldn't want me to, anyway. The future isn't predictable. You can just do everything in your power to make things the best they can be—but you can't control Kendra's life. She'll resent you for it and, pretty soon, you'll resent her as well. Step back. Let her come to you."

"Okay."

A raised eyebrow. "That simple?"

"You make a valid point. I need to learn to give her more space. Who knows, maybe she made all those mistakes because I was clinging on too tightly."

"Well, there's a piece of self-reflection I hadn't anticipated."

I chuckled.

He winked.

And we didn't let go of each other's hand until our food arrived.

Chapter Eight

Aaron

Dinner was splendid, but the walk by the river after was even better.

Noel held my hand as we wandered across the bridge, stopping to look down as the moonlight flitted across the moving water.

I wrapped my arm around his shoulder and tugged him close.

He pressed a kiss to my temple.

This made no sense...and yet nothing had ever felt so right.

I wasn't used to physical attraction. I could objectively look at a man and say he was someone who society recognized as attractive—but I didn't feel anything. Trey sent me an article a while back—about the spectrum of gender, sexuality, and attraction. I figured he was trying to tell me something about himself—so I read dutifully and sat down with him—prepared to deal with whatever he shared.

He wanted to talk about me.

Ugh.

He kept going on about how being gay was only one facet of my life and... To my shame, I'd tuned him out. I did not want to talk about my sex life—or lack thereof—with my then-twenty-year-old brother. I would've accepted anything he had to say about himself. Was prepared to deal with whatever consequences might happen. Although if he told me he was into deeply masochistic behavior and was someone's plaything, I might've panicked. Accepted...and panicked.

As far as I'd been concerned, we didn't need to talk about me. I was a private person—for all he knew, maybe I had twenty lovers.

Yeah, right. In Cataluma? No secrets. Well, I suppose I could've gone to LA. Did on occasion, in fact. I went to gay bars—to hang out and meet people. Never to go home with, though.

"You're thinking so hard, your brain is liable to explode." Noel tapped my forehead. "I thought I was the one with all the problems, and you were the one with his shit together."

I laughed. "Uh, that'd be a hard no." I gazed into his eyes, darker in the moonlight. "There's something about you..."

He licked his lips. "You feel it too, right? Which is nuts because we've known each other twenty-four hours, and you've really only seen my bad side."

That, I questioned. He made it sound so simple, and yet it was anything but. Still, I pulled him in for a hug, reveling in how his body felt against mine. We were about the same height, so when he tucked his head down across my collarbone, I was able to rest my chin on his head.

He clung to me.

I held him.

Something inside my chest expanded in a way I'd never expected.

Finally, he pulled back and met my gaze. "Can we go home?"

I placed a chaste peck on his lips. "Yeah, we can go home."

Our walk was made in silence as we still clasped hands.

We passed a couple who were about my age. Nora was the niece of Jock, now the owner of Making Sweet Music. He'd been in the hospital recently, and she'd come down to take care of things. And the guy looked familiar as well. I seemed to recall he gave lessons to the kids in the summer.

They looked completely into each other, and my heart lurched. I always wanted my friends to find love—I'd just never thought it was in the cards for me.

You think you love Noel?

Of course not.

But could you...?

Aw, shit. Yeah, I did. Eternal optimist I was, I believed some divine intervention had brought this man into my life. I hadn't needed to step in last night. Frankly, I probably shouldn't have. But I'd been compelled. And I could tell myself I'd done it because I didn't want a repeat of the Watson/Wainwright feud, but that didn't ring true either. I'd found Noel oddly endearing and, even from afar, I'd known I needed to step in. I just hadn't foreseen it ending with him sleeping on my couch.

We entered the inn, and Cecelia greeted us with a warm smile. "Have a nice time?"

"Lovely evening. We ate at The Copper Moon."

"Oh." She fiddled with her pen. "Was Paul working? Because he's home from school, right?" She bit her lower lip and waved her hand. "Never mind, stupid question."

I found my flummoxed employee rather endearing. She was several years older than Paul and, as far as I could see, way ahead of him in maturity. Still, the young man was handsome and in law school—

"We saw Paul." Noel grinned. "I have to say, he's pretty darn smart. And handsome too."

Cecelia's eyes flickered.

"Oh, not in that way." Noel laughed. "I mean, he's cute. Not my type. Like at all."

And I nearly asked him what his type was, but he squeezed my hand.

My desk clerk noticed the joined hands and offered a smile. "I'm glad you had a lovely night."

"Anything I need to know?"

She shook her head. "Well, one guest complained about the lobster bisque. We comped the meal. Other than that, things are quiet." She eyed me. "You run a tight ship."

I did, but Cecelia wasn't known for dishing out compliments. She was very much a tell-it-like-it-is person—letting me know when things weren't working and often making suggestions to improve the place. She was only in her mid-twenties, but she was putting her hotel management classes to good use. I'd been lucky to snag her—she could've chosen her work location elsewhere—and certainly, I was sure, Cataluma hadn't been at the top of her list. But her younger brother had leukemia, and Cecelia'd come home to help out her family. I likely wouldn't have her forever.

After a long moment, while I considered asking how her brother was doing, Noel squeezed my hand.

Right. "Well, I'll let you get back to it. You know where I am."

She tilted her head.

Heat rose in my cheeks.

She gave me that secret smile that women seemed to have when they sensed more was going on beneath the surface. And rare were the moments when that applied to me—I was a *what you see is what you get* kind of guy.

Noel and I made our way upstairs, still holding hands.

He finally let go when I pulled out my wallet.

I swept my card and gestured for him to go in first.

He did, flipping on the light as he stepped inside.

After closing and locking the door, I moved to the living room. I turned on two strategically placed lamps, then moved back to turn off the overhead light.

"Setting the mood?"

No missing the teasing note in Noel's voice.

"Sure, if that's what you want to think. The truth is I like to slowly wind down. I try to avoid screen right before bed, and I avoid harsh lights as well."

"Wow. That's like...the mature thing to do." He waggled his eyebrows.

I snickered. "Dare I ask?"

"On my phone or my laptop until my eyes droop. Chronic insomniac—always worrying about all I need to accomplish the next day."

Sounded horrible to me. "After dinner, I write up a list of my tasks so I can forget it and just enjoy a quiet evening."

"Ah, well I have a lot of things to do tomorrow."

"Would you like a notepad?"

"Actually..." He gazed away toward the windows that looked out over the Rio Luminita. In the blackness, there was nothing to see.

"Actually..." I prompted.

He turned back. "I'd like to kiss you again."

Those unfamiliar butterflies were back in my stomach.

"Uh, where?"

Right, because, like, that was the most important thing to know.

He advanced into my personal space.

I held my ground.

He again took my cheeks in his hands.

I held his gaze.

Then, my eyes fluttered shut as he pressed our lips together. He applied just the right amount of pressure as I took in all the things that flitted through my head—his scent, the feel of his hands against my stubble, and, most importantly, the way our bodies pressed together. This time, I opened for him.

Taking advantage of the offer being made, he slid his tongue into my mouth. I'd never been a fan of kissing, but something about this man had me wanting more.

Feeling more.

Demanding more.

He meandered his hand down my neck, across to my arm, and downward still.

I continued to cling to him.

He continued his journey until his hand slid around my waist, and he cupped my ass.

That brought us even closer together.

His hard cock brushed my perking-up one.

A whole new series of sensations bombarded me.

I moaned.

He pulled back. "Too fast?"

"Uh, no."

"Not fast enough?"

"Uh, no."

He tapped my nose. "I don't want to rush you."

"Because you're leaving, right?"

"Partly."

I cocked my head.

"Mostly because I get the feeling, this isn't the norm for you—you're a slow-and-steady kind of guy."

Again, how did he know me so well? Read me so well? "And you're not?"

He winced. "I, uh... Well, for the most part, I don't really do relationships. I mean, I like guys—and I love sex—but I don't do long-term. And the guys I choose aren't into that either. So it works out."

"Haven't you ever met someone who made you want more?"

"Well..."

I waited.

"I met a guy—a business executive like myself—and we were very much about getting naked. But, at some point, we talked. And I was under the distinct impression that wasn't the norm for him either. He needed a shoulder—was going through a rough time—and I'd had some major Kendra catastrophe and...for a night..." He waved it off. "But he had a very strict rule about repeats, and I had to respect that."

"But if he hadn't...?"

"I don't know if it would've worked out. I mean, I would've been willing."

My stomach sank.

"But that was three years ago. Not even a blip on my radar these days."

"So, you've been with a lot of guys?"

Another wince.

"Sorry—"

He again waved it off. "I like sex. I've found other men who feel the same. Do I keep a list? No. Is it an excessive amount? Also no. I practice safe sex, and I enjoy myself—especially when I can please my partner."

"They tell you?" Somehow I wouldn't have pictured that.

He snickered. "It's usually pretty easy to tell if a guy's had a good time. I mean, I suppose you can come and not be satisfied, but most guys are happy to get off."

Beyond my realm of experience.

"Will you...show me...?"

Oh, my God, did I just ask that?

He scrutinized me. "We can have some fun, sure."

I wasn't sure I wanted to know what he meant by *fun*.

But I was willing to find out.

Chapter Nine

Noel

B *old enough?*

Or totally inappropriate?

Huh. Could go either way.

I didn't know Aaron all that well, but I'd figured out enough to know he didn't do casual hookups. Hell, I didn't even get the sense he did a lot of sex. Which was fine. Plenty of guys didn't go that route. Some were quite happy with their hands, and others didn't have the inclination. I knew a few women who, in candid moments, expressed the same thing.

I couldn't really relate. For whatever reason, that I didn't care to examine, both Kendra and I had high sex drives. I liked to use sex as a stress relief—and given how much stress my sister put me through—I pretty much had a consistent cycle of men. Which sounded all kinds of bad. Which was why Shaw was so outside my comfort zone. I'd really liked the guy. He'd sensed that and backed right away.

Lesson learned.

Aaron was different—in every way possible.

"Are you sure I'm not pushing you?"

His grin was wry. "Oh, I'd say you're pushy. But a guy needs to be pushed now and then."

My unease grew.

He smiled, leaned over, and pressed a kiss to my lips. When he pulled back, his dark eyes were almost black with dilated pupils. The low light or sexual desire?

I wasn't sure. "I'd never—"

He pressed a finger to my lips.

This was kind of becoming our thing.

"I know how to say *no*. And I don't know how far I can take this—"

"We won't go any further than you're comfortable. I promise."

"Then I don't see why we can't move this to the bedroom." He winced. "Aw, shit."

I cocked my head.

"I don't have supplies."

Which told me everything I needed to know. "I've got a couple of condoms in my suitcase pocket along with a travel bottle of lube."

He quirked an eyebrow.

"I believe in being prepared."

"Fair enough."

"Why don't we leave the condoms where they are? But I think we can put the lube to good use."

His eyes widened.

I waited as he digested that.

"Uh, yeah, okay."

"Why don't you head to the bathroom? Get ready for bed and then hop in? If you've changed your mind by the time I join you, I'll head out to the couch and we're good."

"I won't change my mind."

Our gazes met. "You can always change your mind. One word and we stop. No recriminations and no regrets."

"Do you have this conversation with all the guys you're with?"

I drew in a deep breath and blew it out. "I...it's kind of understood. Consent is a thing. They all know they can say *no*." And why were we talking about other men?

Because he needs reassurances.

Was I supposed to make up a story to tell him so he'd feel better?

"I'm okay." He scratched his scalp. "It's been a long time. I don't know the rules."

"There are no rules. You do what feels right. And you stop if it doesn't feel good. And you don't worry about what I'll think, because your feelings are the most important."

"That doesn't sound fair."

I smiled. "I'm a big boy. It takes a lot to hurt my feelings."

"That's sad."

His comment had me stuttering. I'd never—not for a mo-ment—thought of it that way. Perhaps because I chose partners who couldn't hurt me. Because I never let anyone get close? Kendra and my father were the only people who could hurt me deeply—I kept all my other relationships shallow.

Have I been missing out?

Perhaps.

But if I had someone back home, then I wouldn't be contemplating how to give pleasure to this amazing man—so that all balanced things out, as far as I was concerned.

I pressed another kiss to his lips. "We're going to be okay." I was going to be okay—because this was just a fling. No way was my heart going to get involved.

He ducked his head shyly then headed to the bathroom.

I made my way over to my suitcase.

Never leave home without it.

I plugged in my phone as I checked it quickly for messages.

Nothing.

How had Kendra and Javier fared today, after they'd left? Had Javier told Kendra about his phone call to our father? Hell, should I have called the man? Nah, if he wanted to reach out, he knew the number. Maybe he needed time for Kendra's rash decision to sink in—I knew I did.

The bathroom door opened, and I caught a glimpse of a naked figure booting from the bathroom to the bedroom.

I smiled to myself. In turn, I closed all the blinds. The ones facing the river probably didn't need to be closed, but better safe than sorry. I wanted Aaron to be comfortable in his own skin. After stripping and putting my clothes in a neat pile, I sauntered into the bathroom. My toiletry kit sat there, and once I'd pissed, I washed my hands and then brushed my teeth. Finally, I took a good look in the mirror. I took care of myself, and my body showed it. And, for the first time in a long while, I cared about what my partner would think about me. I wanted Aaron to find me attractive.

Yet even as I had the thought, I wanted more. I wished he'd be attracted to my mind as well.

Huh, that was new.

Okay, enough dithering. He's had enough time to make up his mind.

I hoped he wouldn't change it, but I wouldn't be upset if he did. Maybe a bit disappointed, but nothing I wouldn't get over quickly.

Again, I sauntered. I entered his bedroom and stopped short.

He lay with his head resting on a pillow. His blanket was pulled up past his waist, giving me only the most tantalizing view of his broad chest. I caught sight of a few crinkly black hairs. My hair was sparse—I'd never been hairy. And, being an egalitarian, I didn't care whether my partner had a pelt or was bare. No, I was more concerned about how to make him come. Then making sure he made me come.

But now...?

I wanted so much more.

Slowly, I advanced. I placed the lube on the nightstand.

He eyed it.

God, was he—

"I've done this before." Words said in a rush.

"Okay." *Take it slow. Let him come to you.*

"I've even done it both ways."

"Okay." I considered. "So have I. When I was younger."

"And now?"

I tried to get a read from him. I didn't care how we did it. Hell, at this point I didn't care whether we did it at all. I itched to touch, and this discussion wasn't conducive to getting and maintaining an erection. "I tend to top. Just what I prefer. But I'm open to any position." I pointed to the lube. "And we're not going that far tonight, okay? I mean, we can talk all you want—if that'll make you feel more comfortable."

"Or we can do."

"Or we can do."

Slowly, he drew back the blanket.

His body was a thing of beauty. He wasn't sculpted—which was totally fine. But he had definition with a broad chest, black hair arrowing downward to his soft belly and, as he revealed the last part of him, a nice cock. It wasn't erect—but it wasn't flaccid either. Not quite a semi, but definite potential.

I licked my lips.

He blinked lazily.

I slid into bed next to him.

When he started to pull up the covers, I waylaid him. He cocked his head.

"I want to look."

A slow nod. Then, his gaze raked up and down my body—almost like he hadn't gotten a good look before.

Nerves?

"May I...?" He held his hand just beyond my body.

I lay on my back and offered myself up.

He moved closer and then, almost reverentially, touched me. His fingers traced across my chest, pausing on my nipples.

They puckered.

He grinned. Then he leaned over and pressed his mouth to one.

My cock sat up and took notice. I didn't want it to become a distraction, though, so I ruthlessly thrust down the need growing within me. It'd never be enough—I could be with him forever and I'd never be sated.

He grazed his hand down my side. When he got to my hipbone, he pulled it back toward my bellybutton. For a moment, he hesitated. Then he trailed his hand down to my bobbing cock, nestled in a thatch of dark-blond curls. Tentatively, he touched.

An electric shock pulsed through me.

So many men had done this before—and yet it felt like the first time.

He stroked lazily. Exploring. Getting to know. Discovering.

In turn, I watched his cock slowly fill and begin to curve up toward his stomach.

After a bit, he released my cock and cupped my balls.

That brought nearly as much pleasure.

He caught my gaze. "You like?"

"I really do." I pointed to his stiffening cock. "May I?"

"Yeah, I think I'd like that."

Slowly, I repeated the same voyage he'd embarked on. I began on his chest, tweaking one nipple, then the other.

He smiled.

I drew my finger down his sternum and dipped my finger into his bellybutton.

He thrust his hips forward.

Impatient?

I liked that. So I continued my leisurely journey downward until I took his cock in my hand. As I stroked lazily, it came to full attention.

He sucked in a breath.

I caught his gaze.

"That feels so good."

Yeah, I knew what he meant. I released him and leaned back to grab the lube. I held it up.

He nodded and held out his hand.

I dribbled some into his palm, repeated the process for myself, then set the bottle aside. I rubbed my palms together the warm the gel, and then I reached for his cock.

After a moment, he did the same.

A little slippery, but I wasn't going to go raw with him. Some guys liked a little discomfort. Some guys liked a lot of pain.

Aaron didn't seem like that kind of guy at all.

His eyes fluttered shut and his rhythm stuttered when I swiped my thumb along his slit. A *Jesus* slid from his lips.

That made me feel pretty good as I continued to stroke him.

He pulled his lower lip through his teeth.

I increased my pace, revelling in the friction.

His hand dropped away from my cock entirely.

Didn't matter. I was solely focused on him—on his desire. I wasn't sure I'd ever been so invested in someone else's pleasure. He needed to enjoy this. If this was the only time we did this, then I needed him to have the best memory possible of that Canadian who passed through his life.

"I'm coming. Oh God..."

He spurted cum all over my hand.

I continued to milk him through the orgasm—wringing out every last ounce of enjoyment that I could from him.

His skin glowed with a sheen of sweat, and his breathing was labored.

I wasn't sure I'd ever seen someone more gorgeous. I glanced around for a box of tissues and found none. Slowly, I let him slip from my hand, and I rose and headed to the bathroom. Ah, a clean washcloth. First, I washed my hands, then I ran the cloth under hot water and headed back into the bedroom.

Aaron lay sprawled, his arm over his eyes. His breathing was still harsh.

I crawled onto the bed and slowly swept the cloth down his belly.

He startled, lifting his arm from his eyes. "Hey, I should—"

"No *should*." I offered a bright smile. "I take it you enjoyed yourself."

"You know I did."

I heard the hesitation. I cocked my head.

He pointed to my deflating cock.

I washed his balls and took special care of his cock.

He moaned.

After I pulled back, I went back to the bathroom to hang the washcloth and then to rinse my hands again. In the mirror, I caught my reflection. My cheeks were hectic with color, and I also had a rosy glow. I couldn't remember the last time a hand job hadn't been a mutual thing—but I didn't feel deprived. I felt invigorated. I felt joyful.

Heading back to the bedroom, I turned off the bedside lamp and crawled in. "Turn on your side. Facing away from me."

"But I should—"

"Shush."

He stilled.

"I have everything I could ask for. Now I want to hold you in my arms."

After a long moment, he complied.

I scooted in behind him and drew our bodies together. Again, I didn't do a lot of spooning, but this felt right. This felt necessary. Slowly, I stroked his chest.

He sighed. "I didn't know it could feel like that."

Wow, hadn't seen that admission coming. "It can be even better. But if that's all we do, I'm happy."

"You're sure?"

I caught the tentativeness in his voice. I pressed a kiss to his shoulder. "I'm sure. Now, sleep."

Within just a few moments, he was out.

A long time passed before I followed.

Chapter Ten

Aaron

A feeling of warm contentment pulled me from sleep.

That and I was too hot.

Oh, the guy behind me might have something to do with that. Noel was plastered to me, with an arm still banded around my chest.

The first light of dawn filtered through the blinds. So probably not even six.

We hadn't stayed up that late last night, and I felt quite sated. Comforted. Embraced.

Alive.

And I could either lie here and examine my feelings—including the fact Trey was probably right when he told me I was demi-sexual—or I could turn the tables on my guest and finish what we started last night. Because not for a single second did I question my attraction to him.

In my mind, I ran through the various options. A hand job would likely be appreciated. A blow job would be better, though, right?

Guys loved blow jobs. I'd given a couple and received a couple and it'd been...fine. Except I hadn't cared about those guys. I'd just known that was expected of me and so I'd done it. Now, though? I wanted to do something that'd bring Noel pleasure.

The other option was digging through his suitcase for the condoms. I'd been fucked before. Again, I hadn't been into it. The guy'd been nice enough, and I'd done my best to enjoy it, but it hadn't been something I'd yearned to do again.

Today, though?

Definite possibility.

But more than I could contemplate.

Slowly, I eased out from under his arm. I held my breath as he resettled on his back.

In repose, he was so attractive. His stubble was thicker and darker than it was a few days ago, and I longed to scratch it with my finger-nails. The morning light trailed a pink streak across his pale skin. Such a contrast to my own.

With deliberate care, I pulled the blanket down. The one he'd tugged over us at some point.

His shaft lay in the nest of curls.

I hadn't spent a lot of time examining his cock before—either last night or on previous occasions when given the opportunity. In a way, I felt awkward as a voyeur. On the other hand, he'd made it clear touching was permitted. He'd allowed me to drink my fill last night.

Gently, making as little movement as possible, I scooted down the bed and positioned myself over him in such a way that I could see his face.

His soft snore made me chuckle.

After consideration, I lightly trailed my finger along his cock.

He stirred, but didn't wake.

Feeling emboldened, I grasped him.

He moaned. And thickened.

Tentatively, I swiped my tongue along the slit.

A groan escaped his lips. But his eyes didn't open.

I repeated the action, tasting the salty tang of precum. This, I could get into. Hesitantly, I licked around the crown. I liked his taste. And his scent was doing all kinds of things to my insides. Inhaling deeply, I grinned. Then, finally, I pulled him into my mouth.

Awkward. I couldn't seem to get the right angle and then I almost choked. I pulled back, but not off.

A gentle hand stroked my scalp. "That feels so good, baby, but only if you want."

I glanced up to meet hooded eyes, bleary from sleep and yet somehow blazing with passion.

He liked this.

So I resumed my ministrations. This time, more slowly, I sucked him into my mouth. I tongued his slit and elicited more moans.

His fingernails raking my scalp increased in speed to accompany my bobbing up and down.

I was pretty sure this wasn't the best way to give a blow job, but he also didn't seem to care.

He grasped my ears, holding me steady. "I'm coming. If you don't want—"

I did want, so I sucked harder. This time I pulled him deep into my throat, not caring that tears were gathering in my eyes and that I couldn't breathe. *Only a moment—then he'll be happy.* And I would be as well.

Cum hit the back of my throat, and I nearly pulled off in surprise, even though I knew it was coming. I did pull back and swallow as best I could. Still, a little dribble went down my chin.

Ew.

Yet he didn't think so.

I popped off, placing a gentle kiss to his cock before he encouraged me to climb over him.

He wiped the spit off my mouth, then yanked me down for a toe-curling, soul-searing kiss.

My nerves sang in pleasure even as my cock lay painful against his belly. I never wanted this feeling to end. My entire life, I'd sought some kind of connection. Now I'd found it—with the one man I couldn't keep.

Might this open the floodgates? Might I finally be able to have sex with random guys?

In my heart, I knew the answer.

Noel was special. He was my unicorn. He was the one man who made me feel things I hadn't believed possible. And how was that? We'd barely been together thirty-six hours, and yet I was contemplating our future. He was busy with work, but surely, he could fly down sometimes. And I could go north, right? Hadn't he said skiing in Whistler? I had competent staff—surely, they could run the place if I took a few weeks off a couple of times a year.

Not enough. It'd never be enough.

"What's going on?"

I pulled back to meet Noel's gaze.

"You went somewhere. Are you regretting this?"

"No." I injected as much feeling into the word as I could.

"Great." He blinked a couple of times. "I just thought..."

"Thought...?"

"Maybe that you were ace. And I didn't want to push you into anything..."

"I don't like labels."

He winced.

"But if I had to find something that fit, I'd say I was demi."

Another wince. "Then we moved awfully fast. I should've given you more time to get to know me. To, I dunno, care about me."

I rested my chin on his chest. "Here's the thing—I do care about you. I care a lot. I mean, it's not love, right?" Even as I said the words, my heart constricted. "Because people don't fall in love in a day."

"Unless your name is Kendra Barker." His grimace was adorable.

I wanted to say that maybe loving a Barker *could* happen in a day. Maybe there was something extra special about him and Kendra. God knows, I'd felt like I'd made a friend mere moments after meeting Kendra. She had that *je ne sais quoi* about her that pulled people in. I hadn't been the least surprised when Javier fell in love with her. "Speaking of Javier and Kendra..."

"Uh, maybe not while I have a hard cock against my hip?"

My erection was waning, but it perked up at being noticed.

He waggled his eyebrows.

I grinned.

"Do you want a blow job or a hand job?"

"Yes, please."

"You pick."

I shook my head. "Surprise me."

And so he did. He worked me into a fever pitch with his clever fingers, and then he took me into his mouth. Then down his throat.

The orgasm hit hard and fast, and as I spurted into his mouth, a feeling of rightness settled over me.

He stroked my hip as he sucked me dry.

I giggled.

The consternation in his expression, with the thunderous eyes, were all for show. He was pleased with himself. And he deserved to be.

We rose, slowly, and headed to the shower.

I wouldn't have believed I had it in me, but he coaxed another orgasm from me. All that wet, glistening skin, touching, licking... Yeah, I came hard.

So did he.

We managed to dry off and dress—both opting for khakis and shirts. The weather was expected to be warm again, but we had our meeting with Miriam Vincent, and we both knew, without an exchange of words, how important looking professional was.

Over breakfast, in the dining room, clearly nerves were setting in with Noel. He ate his French toast—with real maple syrup—but without much enthusiasm.

I, on the other hand, after having expended so much pent-up energy, was famished. I downed an order of eggs Benedict, a side of hash browns, an order of toast with peanut butter and jam as well as a pile of crispy slices of bacon. Managing to coax some bacon into Noel proved a challenge. "I thought all Canadians loved bacon."

He looked at the plate I'd presented him, and offered a weak smile. "Well, vegetarian and vegan Canadians don't."

"Isn't there turkey bacon?"

Arching an eyebrow, he glanced at the plate, and finally took a piece. "Turkey bacon is not vegetarian."

Which I knew, of course. But he smiled ruefully, and I'd take whatever I could get. I wanted to spend the rest of my life making him smile—which made precisely zero sense.

And yet, I still wished.

Chapter Eleven

Noel

Miriam Vincent was a no-nonsense woman who wore a bright-yellow business suit, sensible pumps, and had a riot of red curls that were completely incongruous with the neat-as-a-pin persona of a competent lawyer she portrayed. Her green eyes were incisive on me as I sat across from her large walnut desk.

Aaron took my cold, clammy hand.

Why did I feel like I was being interrogated? Like I'd done something wrong?

Oh, and the woman looked like she was barely out of high school, let alone with Berkley undergraduate and Harvard Law degrees.

I might be Canadian, but I knew I was supposed to be impressed—and I was. And a little intimidated as well, which I wasn't accustomed to.

"Your sister, a Canadian, intends to marry our Javier."

Was she upset, stating a fact, or vaguely amused? The woman had a poker face, and I couldn't tell.

"Uh, yeah, pretty much."

"Well, there are rules for that." She launched into a long explanation with numbers of statutes or something.

I tried to keep up, but my mind wandered. Between the man holding my hand and the sister I was sure was making the biggest mistake of her life, I had too many things going on in my head.

"So you're saying Kendra can stay and apply for a green card?"

Aaron, saving my proverbial bacon. He'd been right—most sane Canadians loved bacon, and the vegan stuff was, frankly, disgusting. A valiant effort, but a massive fail.

"Yes." Miriam tapped her pen on the yellow legal pad where she'd jotted notes. "Obviously she has to abide by the laws in our country. Eventually she'll need to obtain a driver's license and register her vehicle. Her Canadian license is viewed as international, so she's okay for now. I'd recommend he put her on his health insurance—if he has some. Her Canadian public insurance will cease to cover her here. Medical expenses are the primary reason people go bankrupt."

I winced. "If he doesn't have a plan to put her on, I'll secure a private plan for her."

Miriam whistled. "That'll be expensive."

"She drives a motorcycle. Seems to me if she survives a crash, she'll need good coverage."

Aaron squeezed my hand. "Javier has insurance through his business. He'll take care of her."

Miriam nodded her assent. She seemed as convinced as Aaron that Javier was a good guy.

Maybe you can cut him some slack?

Nah. Not yet, anyway.

He'd have to earn my trust, and he was a long way from that—at this point, anyway.

"I'd like to meet with your sister as soon as possible, so we can initiate the paperwork."

"They're not married yet."

The sharpness in my tone had Miriam's gaze snapping to mine.

"Sorry, just..."

She nodded that I continue.

"I'm hoping they might change their minds. They're so young. Well, Kendra's young. And she's not the most responsible person. And I probably shouldn't be telling you this, but if they do go through with this harebrained scheme, then I want someone who's looking out for her best interests. Because I have to head back to Canada soon. I won't be here to make sure she fills out all the forms correctly. Or that she goes to her appointments." *Or that she doesn't get knocked up the moment I turn my back.* Kendra was one thing. Kendra with a baby was another layer of panic.

Aaron squeezed my hand yet again. He seemed to do that a lot.

And it worked. Calm would radiate through him and into me through that tenuous connection. Tenuous because I doubted it'd hold when over a thousand miles separated us.

Miriam rose and offered her business card. Then, after a moment, she offered a second. "Have Kendra contact me as soon as possible."

I rose, took the cards, pocketed them, and shook her outstretched hand. "I appreciate this."

"We both do," Aaron added.

We'd released hands to stand, but he scooped mine up again.

Almost like he couldn't bear to let go of the connection.

I felt exactly the same way.

We exited Miriam's office, walked through the waiting room, and stepped into the bright sunshine.

Her office was on the first floor of a two-story house that was just a couple of blocks from Prospector's Row. The bright sunshine-yellow façade practically matched the woman's suit.

Didn't yellow clash with red hair?

Really, that's what you're thinking about?

"I, uh, should probably text Kendra."

Aaron leaned over to press a kiss to my temple. "I'm sure you've got a few work things to do. Although, if I'm wrong—"

"Shit. You're not wrong. I meant to email my admin and my junior employee."

"So, we go back to the inn. You do that, I'll make sure the place is still running smoothly, and then, after lunch, you can text Kendra. I think it's great that you're motivated to help her, but you don't want to come on too strong."

He was right. I knew he was right. But that didn't make it any easier to swallow. I prided myself on being a man of action—I saw a problem and I dove in to fix it. Occasionally, the incident might call for sober reflection—which I was capable of—but then I'd leap in and do whatever needed to be done. This whole waiting around for someone else to initiate things didn't work for me.

Suck it up.

Yeah, I'd have to get used to this if I was to remain part of Kendra's life. And despite the shitstorm I was expecting, I did want to stay in my sister's life. She meant everything to me. Not to exaggerate—but I'd lay my life on the line for her.

"Do you want me to send up some food?"

Aaron's question startled me, and I shook my head as he opened the door to the inn.

"You've got a coffee maker, right?" I'd consumed a cup at breakfast, and another at Miriam's office. I wasn't sure I needed another cup, but I was definitely craving one.

"I do." He offered a broad smile. "Pods. I'm sure you can figure it out."

Undoubtedly. Terrible for the environment—but efficient when one was a single guy who worked alone.

I headed upstairs while Aaron headed into his back room.

Jason waved to me as I passed, and I waved back.

Aaron hired great people. That said more about him than any pretty words might.

First, I set up the pod, then I set up my laptop on the desk. The alcove had a window that looked out over a copse of trees. I opened it, and birdsong filtered through. I snagged my coffee and settled in. Using the Wi-Fi password Aaron'd written down for me, I quickly connected to his network and was in my email in mere moments.

Great. Strong signal with good speed—things I sort of expected, but was always pleased to find. I'd warned Lionel, my admin assistant, that I'd likely be away on Monday. Even if we'd left Cataluma Saturday night, getting back to Canada in time for me to start working this morning would've been dicey. I shot him off an email, and while I was composing one to my junior employee, April, he replied back that all was well and I should enjoy some time off. That he and April would hold down the fort.

Her reply was much the same, sent moments after I sent mine.

Apparently Lionel'd taken it upon himself to email her to loop her in before I even could.

God, I loved having efficient staff.

I only had one big meeting this week, and I waffled over whether to cancel or to let April take it. She'd been with me eight months and had proven herself over and over again.

Even as I continued the debate, she emailed me the presentation she'd prepared for the meeting.

Huh. I hadn't asked her to do it, as I'd planned to take care of it on Friday. But Friday'd been consumed with driving to California, and I'd thought to get to it today.

I flipped through each slide carefully—scrutinizing and making comments on a notepad I'd retrieved. In some things, I was simply old school. My laptop was always accompanied by a notebook with a pen and a highlighter at the ready.

By the time I hit the last slide, my mind was made up. After collecting the notes, I emailed April and green-lighted her doing the presentation. I suggested she practice with Lionel and get his feedback and, if she was at all concerned, we could do a video chat and she could show me.

She emailed back that she and Lionel had set up a meeting for tomorrow so she could run through things.

God, did they even need me?

Apparently not this week.

And that was just fine with me. I could review a few things and keep on top of emails while Aaron worked, but the rest of the time I could enjoy myself. Stroll around this beautiful town. Maybe hike the local mountains. I hadn't brought my hiking boots, but picking up a spare at the big-box retailer I'd spotted near the highway wouldn't be too tough. I might also pick up some more summer clothes. Spring had been entrenched when I left Canada—still with plenty of those showers in the forecast. Usually by June we were into the warmer weather. Not this year. I took a quick look at the forecast for Mission City.

Rain, rain, and more rain.

And colder-than-normal temperatures.

Not a real incentive to head home after the sunny climes of SoCal.

Someone knocked on the door.

I rose and headed over to open it.

Aaron stood on the other side, holding a tray laden with food.

"Oh, you needed a hand?" I hadn't realized so much time had passed, but a quick glance at the microwave showed noon had come and gone.

"A hand is appreciated." He winked. "But I also wanted to make sure I wasn't interrupting anything."

I held the door for him, then closed and locked it when he moved toward the dining room.

"What did you think you might be interrupting?" I made sure to add a bit of a leer to my voice.

He glanced over his shoulder. Despite his dark coloring, I noted a distinct blush.

Oh, that was interesting. So teasing him about sex was a way to get him blushing. Was I going to employ this or give him a break?

Give him a break. This is all new to him.

"You meant I might be on a conference call."

Aaron blinked several times as if trying to put me into focus. "Yeah, that's what I was worried about. Didn't want to interrupt."

I moved swiftly to him and took his cheeks in my hands. "It's never interrupting—nothing is as important as you."

Way to blurt it out.

His eyes softened, and he blinked again several times. Did he need glasses or—

He leaned forward and kissed me.

My heart soared as our tongues clashed.

He slid his hand down my side, along my flank, and around to cup my ass. Then he ground against me.

Holy Lord, talk about lovely friction.

My cock sat up and took notice as my libido kicked into gear.

He pulled back. "The soup'll get cold."

To hell with the soup. I was ready to drop to my knees and give him a blow job. Or—even better—drag him to the bedroom and fuck him senseless.

Which yanked me right out of my thoughts.

He deserved patience, kindness, tenderness, and—most of all—time. Rushing things would never work. He needed slow and steady.

I needed a cold shower.

Still, the thought of cold soup didn't sit well, so I moved to the kitchen where I grabbed two glasses. I filled them with water, added ice, and by the time I was back at the dining room table, he had everything organized.

He gave me a quick peck to my cheek, then held out my chair.

A guy could get used to this.

I sat and waited until he was seated before picking up my spoon and taking my first mouthful. I glared at him.

He snickered. "Vichyssoise."

"Huh?"

"Cold soup. I mean, we offer warm soup, but this is a favorite that we serve on Mondays. Broth, milk, cream, leeks, onions, and Yukon yellow gold potatoes."

I eyed the concoction. "I'm not sure this is healthy."

"We use less cream because of the potatoes. Go on, it's healthy."

Deciding to take the plunge—but this time being aware of the consequences—I took another sip. Damn, the soup was amazing.

Aaron caught my gaze and grinned. The smile took ten years off his face. Not that he looked as old as I'd figured out he was. But that smile took my breath away.

My phone buzzed with an incoming text.

I hopped up and stalked over to the desk.

—*Can we meet? Javier and I would like to take you out to dinner at The Copper Moon. Aaron could come.* —

"Might you be interested in dinner with Kendra and Javier at The Copper Moon tonight?" I glanced up from my phone to meet his gaze. "I mean, if you don't have plans.

"No plans," he was quick to assure me. "I'd love to." He took a sip of soup while maintaining eye contact.

All right, then.

• *Sure. Does seven work?* —

She sent me back a flurry of emojis. God, she was supposed to be an adult but always responded so childishly.

Belatedly, I realized I should've checked with Aaron.

"Does seven work for you?"

"Of course." Said casually, as if it were the most obvious thing in the world. Likely, if it wasn't, he'd clear the decks of whatever else he had planned, and he'd make sure he was there. His fidelity—his loyalty—was unwavering.

I don't deserve him.

And I don't really have him.

But I'll enjoy whatever time we have.

With that thought, I returned to the table and resumed eating the delicious meal.

Chapter Twelve

Aaron

I tried to let go of Noel's hand as we stepped into The Copper Moon. This meeting was about Javier and Kendra—we didn't need to muddy the waters by proclaiming that we were seeing each other.

Are you seeing each other?

A question I didn't want to contemplate. Pretty much everywhere we went together, we held hands. Twenty years had passed since I'd been close enough to another guy for PDA. And, as much as I'd liked Solomon, it hadn't been our thing. Neither of us had been out—and just the thought of holding hands would've made me want to throw up.

Now? With Noel? I was happy to proclaim to anyone who was interested that we were together. If only for this day—or this week—then so be it. I'd take whatever I could get. I was greedy that way.

He clung to me as we stepped into the restaurant.

Judy greeted us with a huge smile. "Glad to see you gentlemen back here again. Kendra and Javier are in a booth at the back. Menus are on the table."

In other words, she'd escort us if we wanted, but we could also find our own way.

I smiled and guided Noel toward the back.

Kendra and Javier sat on one side of the booth, their hands under the table. Neither moved to greet us.

Odd.

Well, maybe the formality of the dining room at the inn didn't carry through to here. Probably awkward to get out anyway.

I indicated Noel should go in first, and I held myself still as he slid in.

Then I slid in beside him. I rested my hand on the table.

He snagged it.

Well, okay, fair enough.

Kendra's eyes widened.

Javier regarded first Noel, then myself, and then his gaze settled on Kendra.

Finally, she turned to meet his gaze.

"So, uh..." Noel fumbled in his pocket, pulling out Miriam's business card. "We spoke to a lawyer this morning. She's willing to work with you. If you're really set on this marriage thing—"

Could he have added more derision?

Nope, I didn't think he could.

He pushed the card across the table.

Neither of the couple moved to take it.

Noel scowled. "Right, so she's willing to take you on as a client. There's a list of things you can do before you get married, to prepare—"

Simultaneously, Kendra and Javier placed their hands on the table. *Fuck.*

I recognized the exact moment Noel understood what we were witnessing.

"What the hell?"

He might've bellowed that.

I didn't look around. I didn't need to. The Copper Moon was a laid-back joint enjoyed by both tourists and locals.

Someone raising their voice would definitely catch people's attention. And, as often as not, they weren't subtle about their attraction to gossip.

The matching wedding bands caught the light in just the right way as to sparkle. Kendra didn't have an engagement ring with a jewel or anything—but I suspected Javier'd rectify that soon enough. For all that he'd married her within four days of meeting her, he was also a traditional guy.

What does his mother think?

I was curious, but I wouldn't ask. Enough shit was going on at this table without me tossing in questions that weren't germane to this exact situation.

"Look, Noel, I know this was unexpected—"

"Unexpected?" The word burst out of him in a shout. "You've been together all of five fucking minutes and you got married? How is that even legal? Don't you need a license or something?"

This time I did look around. Several people gawked but, upon catching my gaze, turned back to their food. Well, this'd likely become part of Cataluma lore. Right up there with the Watsons and Wainwrights.

Fuck, indeed.

"Five days," Javier countered. "Long enough to know our hearts."

Noel glowered. Anger radiated off him. Well, more like fury. And his normally pale skin was hectic with an abnormal red color—like he'd been out in the sun and was now a baked lobster.

"You're just a kid. You don't know what you want."

Javier's dark-brown eyes flashed. "I hope that comment wasn't directed at me. Begging your pardon, but I'm two years older than you."

Noel knew that, but, in the chaos, had likely forgotten it. He considered himself far more mature than Javier, even though they were very much of the same age and status in life.

"And I'm not a child," Kendra bit out. "I'm twenty-two fucking years old."

"Don't swear."

She plowed on as if not hearing Noel. "I'm old enough to make my own decisions. Old enough to drink—in both countries. Old enough to smoke pot—in both countries."

Noel stuck his finger in Javier's face. "If you've given her drugs—"

To Javier's credit, he didn't swat the digit away.

Good man. I'd have likely done so.

"Marijuana is legal. If Kendra wants to consume it in a safe environment, I'm not going to stop her. I'm not a controlling man. I won't try to dominate her and tell her what to do. She's a smart woman who deserves to make decisions in her life about how she wants to live and what she wants to do."

"Jesus Christ." Noel's ears were puce.

Don't find him sexy like this. That is all kinds of wrong.

Sure. But every once in a while, I liked alpha men. I'd never been attracted to them physically, but I liked the thought of someone taking over now and again.

Javier breathed out slowly. "I'm not religious per se, but I'd appreciate if you didn't take the Lord's name in vain while we're in public."

"But privately it's okay?" Noel's voice dripped sarcasm.

Kendra tapped the table. "You're missing the point." She placed her index finger on Miriam's card and slowly drew it toward her. "I'll call her tomorrow."

I caught movement from the corner of my eye.

Paul, the server, hovered nearby.

Subtly, I shook my head.

He nodded, in obvious relief, and retreated.

Kendra and Javier had glasses of water while Noel and I had nothing. Still, now wasn't the time for a friendly interruption.

"Plus, we have a license."

Javier's assertion caught me off-guard. I couldn't fathom where they'd obtained a license between yesterday at lunch and—

"Vegas." I said the word quietly.

Noel shot me a glance. Then, slowly, he pivoted back to the couple. "You got married in Las Vegas?" Again, no missing the venom.

Kendra tipped up her chin. "So what if we did?"

"Oh, my God, did Elvis marry you?"

Noel clearly meant the question ironically, but the look on the couple's face made it pretty clear that was exactly what'd happened.

I tilted my head in question at Javier, but he studiously ignored my inquiry. Instead, he continued to hold Noel's gaze.

Brave man.

Perhaps also a little reckless. This wasn't the Javier that I knew. That man was logical, reasoned, and very focused. He didn't do things on a whim. Opening High Sierra'd taken a lot of work, and he'd never do anything to jeopardize that. Not that marrying Kendra would put his store at risk...but people's impressions of him would definitely change once they heard about the hasty marriage.

And given the number of people in the restaurant tonight? Word'd be all over town by tomorrow morning.

Hell, I'd bet Javier's ex, Gillian, would have the news in the paper. She loved a good scoop.

"Look, Noel, you have to be reasonable—"

"I absolutely do not have to be reasonable." Noel cut Kendra off. "This would be the textbook definition of me being allowed to be upset."

"Don't speak to her that way." Javier's voice was low, and I didn't miss the warning edge to it. "Kendra's being respectful and telling you about what's happened. And we would like you to be happy for us. But what's done is done. There won't be an annulment, or anything else you might be thinking of."

Noel's jaw ticked.

Ah, Javier'd nailed it.

Noel raised a finger.

Javier's eyes narrowed.

I grabbed Noel's finger and gently lowered it.

His gaze pivoted to mine. His eyes widened in surprise—almost like he'd forgotten I was here.

And that shouldn't have hurt...but it kind of did.

I glanced between Javier and Kendra. "We're going to leave you to your celebration. Your meal is on me as a way of extending my congratulations. Please, enjoy." I grasped Noel's hand. "We're leaving."

With that, I slid from the booth and practically dragged my strong-willed companion with me.

To my surprise, he slid along the bench and practically into my arms.

I placed my arm around his waist and guided him toward the door. Judy's eyes widened.

I didn't want to stop, but I'd made a promise to the newly-weds. "Judy, I'm covering Javier's and Kendra's meals. Whatever they want. I'll come back and settle up tomorrow. Make sure Paul knows—they're not to pay."

She nodded. "Of course, Aaron." I saw the question in her eyes, but she was a seasoned professional—she knew when to intervene and when to stand down.

I appreciated her discretion. Navigating carefully, I soon had us out on the sidewalk.

Noel drew in a lungful of air.

After a moment, I did the same.

We were blocking the door, so I guided him over to a bench.

He plopped down.

Slowly, I crouched before him.

Our gazes met.

To my relief, his color was returning to normal. In the setting sun, he appeared a healthy pink. His pupils, though, were still blown wide.

His sunglasses were tucked into the v of his shirt.

Should I put them on him?

Then I won't be able to see his eyes.

Well, that settled it. If he needed them, he'd say something.

Right?

After a long moment, he blinked.

I held strong.

He closed his eyes, and a tear streaked down his cheek.

Didn't see that coming.

I didn't know him well enough to know what to do. Offer comfort? Ignore the obvious pain? I was just so far out of my element.

When another tear fell, I wiped it away. "Why don't we go home?"

He nodded.

I pulled the sunglasses from his shirt and gently put them on.

He offered no resistance.

I eased up and then tugged him up.

For just one precious moment, I held him close.

He sagged into the embrace.

So much for concerns about PDA.

Eventually, he shuddered.

I wove my arm around his waist, tugged him into my side, and guided us home.

Chapter Thirteen

Noel

I didn't remember walking back to the inn.

I didn't remember walking up the several flights of stairs.

I didn't remember entering the apartment.

I did remember Aaron taking me in his arms and holding me once the door was closed.

He held me.

I clung to him.

Time fell away.

Why am I so upset? It's not my life that's been ruined.

Ruined was such a harsh word, but I couldn't think of an alternative. All the times I'd rescued Kendra—all the times I'd tried to be the perfect big brother—all for naught. She'd thrown away any chance of a stable, normal life by marrying this...guy.

Javier.

I wasn't racist. Far from it. If I had to peg what disturbed me most about this whole clusterfuck, it was the timing. Five days. You couldn't possibly know in just five days that you'd met the person you were meant to spend the rest of your life with. Things didn't happen that fast. You couldn't possibly know the real person. They hadn't revealed themselves.

Maybe the guy had a mean streak. Maybe he hurt puppies. Maybe he cheated on his girlfriends.

None of those seemed probable, but how could I know?

How could Kendra know?

She couldn't. That was the point. She was flying as recklessly into this marriage as she did everything else in life. She rode her motorcycle with abandon. She made decisions without due consideration.

In other words, she wasn't mature enough to make such a life-altering decision.

Aaron continued to hold me as my thoughts spiraled.

Finally, he rubbed our cheeks together. "Why don't we call it a night? I don't know about you, but I'm exhausted."

Sleep? He wanted to sleep?

I couldn't fathom it. "Uh, you go ahead. I'm just going to..." My gaze shot back and forth between the television, my laptop, and my phone.

Fuck.

I needed to call our father. To warn him. Better that he heard it from me—

"You're exhausted, Noel. We were up at the crack of dawn."

Pointing out that'd been his doing—blow job and all—wasn't useful, so I held my tongue.

"But if you want to watch television, that's fine. I'm sure—"

I kissed him. In that moment, I didn't want to watch television. I didn't want to call my father. I wanted life-affirming passion, and I'd do just about anything to get it.

If Aaron'd given me any indication that he wasn't game, I would've backed off.

Far from that, he grabbed me by the shirt collar and dragged me to his bedroom.

I went willingly.

We kissed while unbuttoning each other's shirts.

My hands were clumsy.

He pulled back. "Why don't we undress ourselves and then get into bed?"

"Oh, I like how you think."

He licked his lips.

But I saw it. A shadow passing in his eyes.

Was that regret? Was he doing this for my sake, and not because he wanted it?

Then he snagged my hand and dragged me to the bed.

Okay, then, he was onboard with this.

I must've put my sunglasses down on the table in the other room. Now, I unbuttoned my shirt. Part of me wanted slow and seductive, while most of me wanted skin to skin. What I really wanted was to be inside Aaron, but that was way too soon. Maybe on a future date. Or maybe not. Some guys weren't into that, and I was totally fine with it if that was the case.

Huh.

As I shucked my pants, I considered that thought. I'd never been with a guy and not had anal, but for Aaron, I'd happily forgo that.

We'd take this at his pace.

I yanked down my briefs as he removed the last of his clothing, and we placed it nicely on the chair.

Then we turned to each other.

As turned on as I was by him, my cock wasn't really interested.

He sported a semi, and I was prepared to bring him pleasure, but he snagged my hand as I reached out. He pressed it to his chest. "I, uh, just want to snuggle."

I gazed into his dark-brown eyes—nearly black in the dark. Yeah, I felt the same way. "That'd be perfect."

We crawled into bed, and I luxuriated in the crispness of the linen. *Must be nice to have housekeeping at your door*. Although...that meant his staff would be privy to his nocturnal activities.

He didn't appear concerned. In fact, he held open his arms. "Turn on your side, I want to cuddle."

Worth arguing about? I did very little cuddling in my life, but I was always the big spoon. Even when the guy was bigger—which wasn't often—I'd take the lead. Still, Aaron asked so little of me that I couldn't refuse him this. I turned on my side, facing away from him, and he pulled me into his arms.

A muscular arm banded around my chest. His hair tickled my back. His thighs pressed against mine. And...

"You know I can take care of that."

A low rumble of a chuckle. "I'm able to as well. Truthfully, I'm kind of enjoying this—this edging."

Proof, if I needed it, that he didn't sport erections often.

That knowledge kind of glowed in my chest. I could do this to him. For him. Prove that he could feel sexual attraction—if he made a deep emotional connection first.

Forty-eight hours. I'd known the man forty-eight hours. My heart was already gone. Well, I wasn't positive. But I'd never felt this way about anyone—protective, aroused, giddy... Never all those in that combination.

Aaron kissed my shoulder and, within a few moments, his erection lessened. Not long after that, he drifted off to sleep.

My mind, however, would not shut down. Aaron, Kendra, Javier...my father. All needed something from me. Or wanted something from me. Was I even capable? Could I be strong for all of them?

Aaron was proving to be the easiest—he placed so few expectations on me. He didn't want to see me upset. Clearly, he'd do everything in his power to lighten my burden.

But was it fair for me to ask him to take on so much? Because he'd likely feel obliged to watch out for my sister and her new husband.

That thought still gave me nightmares.

And Aaron might try to balance a relationship with me. A thousand miles separated us. I simply couldn't ignore that fact.

Slowly, though, sleep dragged me under.

Darkness still shrouded the room when I woke.

I didn't need to check the clock radio to know we were close to dawn.

Hey, today was the summer solstice.

Or close to it.

Plenty of daylight to drive in.

Because my mind was made up—I needed to leave.

I could tell myself I was leaving for Aaron's sake. I didn't want him to sink any deeper into this relationship. I could tell myself I was leaving for Kendra's sake. If I didn't run into her in this small town, then there wouldn't be another confrontation. Hell, I could even tell myself I was doing this for our father's sake. He deserved to hear the news about his only daughter in person. And since Kendra and Javier wouldn't be jetting off to Canada any time soon, that left the task to me.

She's probably already called him.

Well, that was true.

Which left the true reason was I leaving. For my own sake. I mightn't have ever been in love before, but I could safely say I was falling for Aaron. Part of me was ready to hand over my business to Lionel and April and let them take over. Part of me envisioned staying here—in Cataluma—and building a life with Aaron.

Absolute fucking insanity. You really need to get your head examined.

I tried to extricate myself from Aaron's firm grasp.

He mumbled, "Don't go."

Oh, how I didn't want to. I wanted to slide my hand between our bodies and jerk him off. I wanted to guide his hand to my own interested cock and have him bring me to climax. Most of all, I wanted an intimate connection to bond us.

Which was why I had to leave.

Slowly—carefully—I disentangled us.

He curled into a ball, shifting so his head rested on my pillow.

So he could smell my lingering scent?

That warmed my heart and tore a piece of it away at the same time.

I fumbled in the dark as I searched for my clothes in the pile—trying to sort out what was mine and what was his.

He flipped the lamp on.

My eyes watered in the sudden light.

Or so I told myself.

I turned to face him.

He'd propped himself up against the headboard. His expression was neutral, but I caught the flash of hurt in his eyes. "Were you going to say goodbye?"

"I, uh, thought it'd be better this way."

Clearly he was unconvinced, as his brow knitted. "Is this because I won't have sex with you?"

I dropped the clothes I'd managed to sort. "Oh, my God, no."

He pulled the sheet up to his chest. "Because we can, you know. I mean…"

Jesus. I crawled onto the bed until I came close to him. Close enough to touch, but I didn't dare. "I would never—ever—leave someone because they weren't willing to do anal. I'd demand to know whatever gave you that idea, but I know the pressure out there on gay men. On lesbians. Hell, on everyone. Society makes penetrative sex out to be amazing. That it's the solution to every rocky relationship. That you can't have a solid foundation without it." I scratched my scalp. "That's all bullshit. I know it, and I hope deep in your heart that you do as well."

He blinked several times.

My heart took a knock.

Pushing aside my doubts, I advanced toward him.

He didn't retreat.

I placed my hand on his cheek.

He turned into the touch.

Mind made up, I leaned forward. I braced one hand on his muscular chest while I kept the other one firmly on his cheek. Then, finally, I bent to press our lips together.

He grabbed me by the back of my neck and dragged me forward. Into his arms. Into the kiss. Into the shelter from the storm racing in my mind.

Here—right now—I could forget all my troubles and just sink into the oblivion he offered.

Moving restlessly below me, he bucked up—as if seeking friction.

I meandered my hand down, under the covers, and unerringly encircled his cock.

He inhaled sharply.

Nailed it. I slid my thumb over his slit to gather a bead of precum. I streaked it down his length. *Not enough*. No, I needed lube. I pulled away to reach the nightstand, but he pulled me closer. "Baby, I need to get lube."

The moment understanding dawned, he shifted to give me access. I opened the drawer, snagged the lube, and closed the drawer again.

While I did that, he tugged the covers down to reveal the body I admired so much. His cock lay against his belly, with a tiny dribble of precum. His balls hung heavy, and I salivated.

I met his gaze. "You sure you don't want a blow job?"

He shook his head. Then he opened his palm, and I understood.

I dribbled lube on his hand and then placed some on my palm as well. I tossed the bottle back on the nightstand, then lay beside him.

Our gazes met.

He broke away first, looking down to where our cocks lay—mere inches apart. He grasped mine.

I held back the gasp. I'd done this so many times—and yet this felt like the first. The first time with him. The first time with someone who held my heart in the palm of the hand that stroked my cock.

As he settled into a rhythm, I took him in my hand. He was smooth, rigid, and warm.

My soul ached. I felt the pain from the top of my head to the tips of my toes.

Stop with the melancholy—get him off.

Possibly easier said than done, but I was someone who could focus when necessary. Put my head down and accomplish any task. So I approached this with the enthusiasm and vigor it required.

Aaron's eyes rolled back and his lids fluttered shut. His cock jerked in my hand.

That easy?

Apparently so. His jerks of my cock were erratic and ceased altogether when he came. His cum erupted over my hand and splashed across my thighs and down to the mattress.

Oh well, he had housekeeping to deal with that problem.

That thought brought a smile to my lips. Despite everything, I instinctively knew Aaron had people in his life who'd take care of him. He wouldn't be alone.

He cleared his throat. His eyes shot open, and he met my gaze.

A slow smile crossed his lips. He tightened his grip on my cock.

As much as I wanted to roll my eyes back and let them close in bliss, I held his gaze. *Does he see how much this affects me? How much I want him? How much I need him?* Part of me mourned that I'd never find out—because I wasn't sticking around to ask him.

He swiped his finger along my slit.

My toes tingled.

He continued his strokes with renewed vigor. His eyes conveyed a message, but my brain was too scrambled to receive the signal.

The orgasm built within me, but crashed so suddenly that I didn't have time to warn him.

His grin warmed me as he continued to gently milk me through my orgasm.

I felt cherished. Cared for.

Loved.

I shut my eyes, but not before a tear leaked out. God, this was the second time I'd cried before him. *What must he think?* I wasn't a crier. After my mother died, sure, but not since then. I'd sworn those were the last tears I'd ever shed.

Aaron pressed his lips to my cheek where the tear'd tracked down.

My heart broke.

Shattered into a million pieces.

Chapter Fourteen

Aaron

I'd closed my eyes after the mutual hand job and pretended to go back to sleep. He didn't want me to see him leave—I had to respect that. Plus, what was there left to say? I'd made it perfectly clear to him that he was welcome to stay for as long as he wanted. Hadn't he said something about taking a vacation? I'd assumed he'd at least stay the week. Maybe if he had...

My mind shut down that train of thought. I wasn't ready to go further with him. Might never be. So maybe things were better ending now rather than carrying on and ending with recriminations later.

He said he didn't care.

Yeah, he had. And, in that moment, I'd believed him.

But guys lied all the time. Or at least that was my experience.

Twenty years is a long time.

And I'd never felt for them the way I felt for Noel.

Which made his departure all the more painful.

When I heard the snick of the front door lock, I slowly rose. He'd shut off the bedside lamp, but I flicked it back on.

Five-twenty.

The sun would crest soon.

I stripped the bed and dropped the sheets in a pile. Then I headed to the bathroom for a good scrubbing in the shower. That chore accomplished, I put on some toast while I dug out my leathers.

Forecast today was for beautiful weather, and I hadn't ridden in some time. Therefore, today was the perfect day to dust the motorcycle off and take it for a spin. Unlike Kendra and her Harley, I favored the sportier Kawasaki. In electric blue.

Mechanically, I ate toast with peanut butter and strawberry jam. I'd have thought to be sick of the stuff by now, but I never was. Except now strawberries would always come with the memory of Noel—and that thought hurt a lot.

I put the plates and cutlery in the dishwasher, did a quick sweep of the place, grabbed my helmet, and headed out the door. I put the tag to request housekeeping on my door. Yeah, Lynne'd been through my place yesterday. Yeah, she'd question it in her mind. But she'd clean the place spotless, change the sheets, and I wouldn't have any reminders of Noel when I came home.

Dream on.

Well, I was allowed to pretend.

I kept my motorcycle in a shed at the back of the parking lot. I popped the lock, opened the door, and breathed a sigh of relief. Not that I'd worried that my baby would be there—it always was. But that I'd see it and not want to ride.

Baby.

Noel'd called me that. And if anyone else had tried, I'd have rebelled. I would've put the fool in his place. No one used a diminutive on me.

Or a pet name.

I eased the bike onto the asphalt of the parking lot.

You liked it.

Fuck.

Yeah, I had. I really had. Somehow, I was certain he didn't do that with his other guys. Well, maybe he did, and I was being naïve.

Nah. Something in those baby blues had convinced me I was the only one. I was special.

And yet he left.

Fuck.

I hauled my leg over the motorcycle and settled myself. I wasn't thrilled about starting the engine so early, but I had a good muffler. I wondered how far Mission City was to the ocean. British Columbia was a big-ass place, and only a small chunk of the population even lived on the ocean. I'd look up Mission City on a map, at some point.

Maudlin?

Yep. No point denying it.

The dawn chased me as I headed west. At a stoplight, I turned my head to gaze back at the blazing pink, purple, and blue sunrise. I faced forward just in time for the light to turn green. Soon, I passed over the highway and continued my westward trek. Not too long after that, I spotted the Pacific. I found a place to pull off where I could park my motorcycle and then gaze out over the massive ocean. At times, I couldn't fathom the size. Aside from my time in LA at school, and when I'd lived with my grandmother, I'd been in Cataluma my entire life. Had never done a run to Mexico. Never headed north to see the sequoia trees in the redwood forest. Had never headed farther inland—to Vegas or some such.

Nope. I stuck to my hometown like glue, with zero regrets.

Except, if I'd been more mature, maybe Noel would've...

Don't go down that road. That road leads to Hell.

In my mind, at least. I could *what if* the scenario to death, but it didn't change the fact he was gone, I was alone, and—truthfully—nothing had changed in my life. I'd still run the inn. I'd still have friends in town. I'd still watch out for my neighbors and strangers.

I'd also know a small part of my heart resided with a man more than a thousand miles away.

After putting my helmet back on, I mounted the motorcycle and pointed it in the direction of home. I could go north and check out the sights. Or I could go south and visit my grandmother. No, better not. She knew me better than anyone—and she'd see I was upset.

Pointing toward the east, I took off. The sun was higher now as morning was well and truly entrenched. Another beautiful day.

I hope Noel has good weather all the way home. I also hoped he didn't overdo it and stopped to take breaks and to stay overnight somewhere. I hoped he'd text and—

Fuck.

I didn't have his cell phone number.

And he didn't have mine.

Oh, my God, what a monumental oversight. I figured we had time, right? Time to get to all the little things that couples did—like exchanging phone numbers. I knew how much he liked hand jobs, but I knew nothing about where he lived. What movies he loved. What made him sad. What brought him joy.

You could ask Kendra.

I could.

But I wouldn't.

Noel deserved privacy—if he wanted me to know those things, then he would've said them.

Time.

We'd needed more time.

I hadn't asked if he'd come back.

He hadn't asked if I'd come to Canada.

So that left us precisely where we'd been Saturday night—strangers. Two lost souls.

Except, for this brief respite, we'd found each other.

And as much as my heart ached right now, I'd get over it. I'd move on with my life. And maybe, in time, I'd find someone else.

Time.

I needed time to get to know someone. I was capable of sexual attraction—with the right person. One man had come along. Surely another might.

The snicker escaped as I crossed the bridge leading back into Cataluma.

After I'd put the motorcycle away and locked the shed, I headed into the inn—helmet in my hands.

Jason caught my eye and pointed to the sitting room.

Curious, I turned that way and headed in.

Kendra sat on one of the antique chairs. The least-comfortable one, no less. When she caught my eye, she rose. After a moment gazing into my eyes, her composure slipped a little.

Just a little.

Then she blinked, straightened her spine, and flashed a smile.

A tight smile—but a smile, nonetheless.

"What can I do for you, Kendra?"

"Noel's gone?"

I nodded.

"Do you know if he spoke to our father?"

I shook my head. "I don't know."

This time, she nodded. Drew in a deep breath. "Javier and I intended to do it today, but something's going on with his mother, and he's had to leave town unexpectedly."

"Is Millie okay?"

Kendra winced. "I might've just said too much."

I glanced around the sitting room, confirming we were alone. I considered inviting her to sit on the couch, but ears could always catch what was being said. "Why don't you come up to my apartment?"

She cocked her head.

"Oh, I live on-site."

"Yeah, okay."

Together, we mounted the stairs.

To my relief, the housekeeping-request card was gone and, when we stepped into the apartment, the only smell was a light lavender fragrance that Lynne used because she knew I liked the scent. She used unscented products in the other rooms.

Kendra walked in and made a slow circuit of the open space. Then she pointed to the first door.

"Bathroom."

And the second.

"Bedroom."

She tapped her finger against her lips. "Should I ask where Noel slept?"

Jesus, that wasn't private or anything. I was about to answer *the couch* when she held up her hand.

"Never mind. That was way too personal." She scratched her nose. "I thought he liked you. He left because of me, didn't he?"

Here, I could be honest. "I don't rightly know. He didn't enumerate the reasons. He took off just before sunrise. You might want to call him tonight to make sure he's stopped and safe."

Her laugh was bitter and grated the wrong way. "I'm the last person he wants to hear from."

I wanted to protest, but she wasn't wrong. So many unresolved issues remained between the siblings. I'd hoped to help them work through some of them before Noel left. On that count, I'd failed. Or fallen short. I couldn't be too hard on myself—he'd made the decision to leave.

"Can I get you something to drink? I'm parched and am going to grab a lemonade."

"Lemonade would be brilliant." She indicated my outfit. "How about I pour the lemonade while you change? You must be hot."

I was. And sweating. "Do you mind if I have a quick shower?"

She shook her head.

As she headed to the fridge, I went into my bedroom. I'd known the bed would be made and all evidence of last night would be gone—but seeing it reassured me. I stripped, hanging up my clothes. Then I snagged a bathrobe and put it on. Finally, I grabbed fresh clothes.

When I exited the bedroom, heading to the bathroom, Kendra was on the couch, totally absorbed in her phone.

I took close to the quickest shower on record. Since my hair was practically shorn, drying it took only moments. I reappeared just a few minutes after having headed in—clean, respectable, and noticeably cooler. I grabbed the glass Kendra'd left for me on the dining room table and headed to the couch.

Kendra scooted over to give me plenty of space.

As I had with Noel, I positioned myself so I could see her. "What's up?"

She scrutinized me. No other word for it. "I wanted to get to know you better."

Huh?

I cocked my head in question.

"If you're going to be part of Noel's life, I feel like we should get to know each other."

After taking a sip of lemonade—to give myself time to think—I met her gaze. "I'm not *in* your brother's life. We spent a couple of days together. Most of that time, he was worried about you."

She winced.

"Not in a bad way," I was quick to clarify.

Again, she met and held my gaze.

"Well, okay, in a big brother kind of way. I worry about my younger brother, Trey, all the time."

"I hear he's a good kid."

"He's a great kid. But I helped raise him—so I'm entitled to worry."

"Like Noel raised me."

Huh. "I'd never thought of it like that. I guess, yeah, your brother and I have that in common. Worrying about a younger sibling is the elder's prerogative. But it's more than that. You and Noel lost your mother at a tough age. Trey was in the same boat. All of us had absent fathers. But we figured it out. We found a way to make it work."

"Do you still run interference in Trey's life?"

Ouch.

Be honest with her.

"Trey's really mature for his age. He's almost finished college—he's on his way to making a good life for himself."

"While I'm not."

Tread carefully.

"I don't know you well enough to make that determination. I like the idea of us getting to know each other better. But from what I've figured out, Noel's always going to be protective of you. I'll be honest, if my younger brother came to me and told me he was marrying someone he'd known for four days, I'd likely have lost my shit as well. And not that it should make a difference—but it does—he's a guy. There are plenty of risks and pitfalls for a guy, of course, but things are more dangerous for women."

She planted her hands firmly on her hips.

My mother flashed to my mind. I hadn't planned to go there, but I'd opened the can of worms. "My father was abusive. We're talking verbal, physical, psychological—he tried to destroy my mother at every turn. I've never completely understood why. Except to say the man was truly fucked up. And, even after he left, my mother was never right. Eventually..." I couldn't do it.

Kendra waited.

You have to.

"Eventually life wore her down. She killed herself when I was twenty-six. By then I had a six-year-old brother whose mother was an addict and whose father had abandoned us. But, really, I'd lost her before then. My grandmother practically raised me, and I owe her everything." I glanced around. "My mother had an inheritance that my father was never able to touch—another sore spot in their fraught relationship—and I got it when she died. I bought this place. And I did my best to try to take care of Trey. He turned out all right, so I guess I didn't do badly."

Kendra glanced around. "You raised him here?"

I shook my head. "We had a little house. When he moved out, and needed money for college, I decided to rent the place out and move here. The money all goes to his education."

She whistled. "That's dedication."

"Isn't that what Noel did for you?"

Her eyes widened. After a moment, her mouth opened. No sound came out. She shut it. Then tried again. Still, no words.

I took her hand. "Look, Kendra, this isn't a criticism of you. You're not Trey. I'm not Noel. We've done our best and, given everything, I think we've done okay. For what it's worth, I approve of your marriage to Javier. Might I have suggested you wait a few weeks? Sure. Do you have my unconditional support? Yes to that as well."

She squeezed tight. "I'm sure I didn't make a mistake, but if I lose Noel..."

"You're not going to lose Noel." I leaned over to deposit my lemonade on the coffee table. Then I tucked a lock of her hair behind her ear—away from her eye. "He's going to come around. I promise."

"Do you really have the right to make that promise?" Her blue eyes shone with unshed tears.

Truth or lie?

"You are the most important person in his life. He'll get over the anger. You'll prove this wasn't a mistake, and he'll come around. I promise."

And I might've had my fingers metaphorically crossed behind my back.

She launched herself into my arms.

I caught her easily.

"My brother's a fool."

I wasn't going to argue.

Chapter Fifteen

Noel

By Friday night, I was ready to drop. My two-day trip home had lasted well into the second night as I'd gotten snarled in Seattle traffic and then stuck at the border which had been closed because of an *incident*.

I hadn't asked.

April had been, rightly, surprised to see me Thursday morning. She offered to give up the presentation spot, but I kept my word and let her have it. And, thankfully, she nailed it.

We signed the contract late Friday afternoon.

Another satisfied customer.

And, I decided to let her take the lead with the account.

She'd earned it.

Lionel'd kept everything running smoothly and, to my immense relief, my inbox hadn't been flooded with issues or complaints. Far from it—most of my clients hadn't even noticed I was gone.

As I stared at my nearly empty fridge, I winced. I lived on takeout. Always too busy to cook. Always too much going on to take care of myself. Always too stressed about Kendra to consider I might need pampering once in a while.

Oh, and I still reeled from my dinner last night with our father.

Kendra'd called him, and he'd been delighted. In fact, he believed I was seeing him so we could celebrate.

I disabused him of the notion.

He wasn't pleased.

I left before dessert.

C'est la vie.

Sighing, I got online and ordered pizza. Marginally healthier than some of the other options, and I'd have plenty of leftovers for the weekend.

As I waited, I scrolled thought notifications on my phone.

My finger hovered over the hookup app I loved to use.

I shouldn't.

But man, could I use some stress relief.

After a long moment, I swiped.

The first few guys didn't do it for me. None were a beautiful Black man with gentle dark-brown eyes.

Then I caught sight of a guy who did sort of do it for me. Dark-blond spikey hair, dark-brown eyes, and just the right kind of slender.

Not muscular—solid and cuddly.

Jesus, get over him already.

My finger hovered for several long moments before I sent a message.

While I waited for my pizza to arrive, I changed into a pair of jeans and a Henley. So much for summer weather—today felt more like early spring or late fall weather. I wasn't going to turn on the heat in the house, but I wondered about whether or not we'd have a repeat of the heat-dome summer or the summer after that, which'd been slow to start and brutally hot at the end.

My phone buzzed.

Okay, so this guy was interested in meeting.

Tonight.

At the Grand Hotel.

At nine o'clock.

At room 309.

Well, that worked for me. I loved it when guys took the initiative and made all the arrangements. I presumed I'd be paying, but that wasn't an issue. The contract April'd just signed would bring in big bucks. My house was nearly paid off, my business was in good shape, and the trip to California—despite the horrendous cost of gas for my SUV—had barely made a dent in my wallet.

So why are you contemplating what might be involved in moving to California?

I shoved that thought aside. I wasn't thinking about it.

Or so you tell yourself.

The pizza arrived, so I chowed down. I stored the leftovers in plastic containers in the fridge and headed for the shower. I didn't really need it, but I liked having my bits clean.

Refreshed and ready to go, I drove to the Grand and parked. I was a few minutes early, so I sat and watched the entrance until I spotted the guy entering. He wore a pair of khakis, a shirt, and...a scarf? Not a winter one, but definitely a signature piece of some kind. If I had to pick a word, it'd be preppy.

And since I didn't care about how he looked, just how he liked to be fucked, I exited my car and headed in. I had plenty of lube and condom packets in my pocket.

As always, the Grand felt shabby. She needed a renovation—or just some decent upkeep. And a good marketing budget. The two chain motels and hotels in town did way more business than this historical site, and that disappointed me. This place had so much potential—most of it unrealized.

I headed up the stairs to the third floor—not trusting the old elevator that was likely older than my father. When I got to 309, I hesitated.

Am I ready for this?

You've never hesitated for a hook-up before.

I've never had a man in my life.

But I didn't have a man. I'd walked away from that man before my heart got involved.

Sure, just another lie you tell yourself.

I ended my internal monologue with an admonition to *fuck off.*

Then I knocked on the door.

The man who opened it was much as his photo portrayed him. His hair was a little shorter and spikier, but the rest was as advertised. Slim, handsome, and with soft dark-brown eyes.

Which made me think of another pair.

Oh, my God, don't go there.

How could I not?

The man ushered me inside. He'd dropped his scarf on the desk, unbuttoned several buttons, and rolled up his sleeves. He'd also turned down the bed.

Despite having done this numerous times over the past ten years, I still wasn't sure of the protocol. Were we just going to do it? I was okay with that. Or did he want a bit of chitchat? I was okay with that as well. Whatever he wanted, I was down for.

He moved to the desk and opened a cooler bag I hadn't seen him arrive with. "Soda? I don't bring booze, but if you'd like, the liquor store is attached to the—"

"Soda sounds great." I never drank alcohol. Even if I was the bigger guy, I never took intoxicants.

He produced a cola, a sparkling water, a fizzy orange drink, and a root beer.

I pointed to the last one.

He grinned and handed it over.

I cracked the can and took a sip. I hadn't realized how parched my throat was.

"My name's Anderson."

"Noel."

He stared for an uncomfortably long time.

I was Mission City born and bred, so people knew me. I often went farther afield for my hookups—Chilliwack, Maple Ridge, Abbotsford, and even as far as Vancouver.

After what felt like forever, he grinned. "Shaw."

"Huh?"

"You know my boss, Shaw Montgomery."

Oh, Jesus.

The one hookup where I'd contemplated asking for a second round. I always got the feeling that Shaw'd sensed that and had bolted. Yet... "Your boss tells you about his, uh, dates?"

Anderson guffawed. "Uh, not usually. Let's just say you made an impression. And he was surprised he didn't know you since you two were about the same age. He figured you went to different high schools."

"I went to Hatzic back when it was a secondary school."

"Ah, he went to Mission City Collegiate."

"He mentioned me?"

Anderson continued to scrutinize me. "He might have. I also keep his calendar and have access to his phone."

"Holy shit." I didn't hold back my surprise. "I have a highly qualified admin assistant whom I trust implicitly, but he'd never have access to my personal phone—let alone be permitted anywhere near my dating apps."

He grinned. "Well, he'd played a nasty trick on me...I might've been seeking revenge." He buffed his fingernails on his shirt. "Unfortunately, he's happy and with someone, so my nefarious plans didn't have the same effect."

"You say that almost like it's a bad thing."

Another hearty laugh. "I love Shaw like a brother and adore his boyfriend—soon-to-be-husband Damien—but I have no scruples."

"Good to know."

He waved me off. "You're golden—completely safe with me. I'm into discretion. And leather daddies, but I was willing to make an exception for you."

I had no idea how I felt about that. Flattered? Annoyed?

Indifferent?

He advanced into my personal space. "Why don't you have a seat on the bed?"

I eyed my root beer. "Should I undress?"

He pushed me lightly until I sat on the edge of the bed.

I totally could've resisted him, but something told me this was important.

After a long moment, he sat in the desk chair. The thing could not possibly have been comfortable, but he didn't show any discomfort. "Who is he?"

"Who is who?" I tried for confused, but even as I said the words, the lie twisted deep in the pit of my stomach.

"I've been doing this a long time. I adopted my niece when she was nine months old. So I've been a single parent since I was twenty-two. These escapes—" He waved his hand around the room. "—are all I get."

"You don't do serious?"

He shook his head. "I'm dedicated to Adele."

"How old is she?"

"Precocious thirteen. Heads to high school in the fall."

"And she would mind you dating?"

He tapped his finger against his chin. "Possibly not. Probably not. But I've never met someone I wanted to bring home. Someone who might upset the relationship I have with her. She's my daughter, and her happiness is all that matters."

I understood what he was saying, but surely twelve years of hookups had to weigh on someone.

Of course, I'd been doing them for eight. Would I be the same four years from now? A little cynical. A little jaded. A little lonely. "Okay, so what does that have to do with me?"

"Shaw liked you. But you scared him. He was deep into running the company he inherited when his father died. Barely twenty-four and thrown into the deep end. His hookups kept him sane."

Again—not sure whether to be flattered or annoyed—and still not seeing what this had to do with me.

"When he met the right person, he knew. And yeah, the relationship didn't come easy. Damien is a great guy, but he came with a lot of baggage." He leaned back. "Something tells me this guy you're running from has baggage."

"Not as much as me," I muttered.

Anderson didn't crow. He merely nodded thoughtfully. "I get it. I really do. But you should be talking to him instead of here, contemplating fucking me."

He was right.

And... *Shit.* "I was never going to fuck you, was I?"

"I'm easy—but I don't poach in other people's forests. This guy has your heart. I saw it the moment I opened the door to you."

"You couldn't have—"

"In your eyes, Noel."

This was the first time he'd used my name. The effect was sobering.

"What do I do? He's in California. I'm in Canada. He has a business there. I have a business here. The whole thing was just a fling. He'll have forgotten me by now."

Anderson pursed his lips. "Something tells me that you're more memorable than you think. Shaw remembered you—and that's saying something."

But I doubted any of the other guys over the years had.

Yet, even as I had the thought, I remembered Aaron's kisses. His unschooled touches. His wide-open heart.

"I've made a mistake."

"Only if you don't go after what you want." Anderson rose. "We can cuddle in bed, if you'd like that, but only as friends. I think you need one, and I can always use more."

Part of me was tempted. I had so little meaningful touch in my life. But the other part of me felt it'd be disloyal to Aaron. Until I was honest with him—and found out once and for all whether we could make things work long distance—I couldn't be with anyone else.

I rose, then held out my hand.

Anderson hopped out of the chair and pulled me into a hug. For such a small guy, he was strong.

I nearly spilled my drink.

He kissed my cheek.

His stubble rasped mine.

"Go get your man. And let me know how it goes."

I placed the drink on the desk. "I will."

This feels like the beginning of what might be a wonderful friendship.

Then, in turn, I kissed his cheek.

And sped out of there.

Chapter Sixteen

Aaron

As I pulled my motorcycle into my grandmother's home in LA, a little pang shot through me. I'd been far enough into adulthood that losing my mother—even to suicide—shouldn't have had the impact on me that it did.

But it had.

And, by then, I'd brought Trey to live with my grandmother, even though she wasn't blood kin. She'd taken him in without a moment's hesitation until I could get my shit organized up in Cataluma.

As soon as I'd secured a house and spent the bulk of my inheritance on the inn, I'd given Trey the option to either stay in LA or come live with me.

He'd chosen me. Then had returned to my grandmother's house while doing his degree at UCLA. Now he was back in Cataluma.

I loved having him close.

He still hadn't decided what he wanted to do with his life, but, at twenty-two, he had all the time in the world. He was a good kid, and I trusted him to do the right thing.

My grandmother stood at the open door as I got off my motorcycle. She'd likely heard it. But she moved slower these days—albeit being a spry eighty-eight.

I must've been sitting and contemplating longer than I realized. I went into her arms.

The petite woman's strength never ceased to amaze me. She no longer mowed her small patch of grass, but she did just about everything else in the house—much to my consternation.

I paid a local kid to drop by.

I told him I worried about her in her golden years.

I told her I worried about him and that he needed the cash.

Both statements were correct. Both statements were also self-serving.

Whatever. I didn't have to constantly worry about her, and the kid was planning to attend a local college and was just sixteen, so I figured I had his loyalty for another six years or so, and I was happy to contribute to his schooling.

Win/win.

Nana smacked me on the shoulder. "You haven't been down for a while."

True. But I'd brought her up to Cataluma for a visit at Easter.

Over two months ago.

Guilt.

I need to do better.

She pointed to the sofa. "I'll get you a lemonade."

I knew better than to argue. I tucked my helmet into her front hall closet and made my way over to her floral couch. The thing was older than me, but was still pristine. She only allowed *guests* to sit on it. Family hung out in the family room.

When I'd been elevated from family to guest, I wasn't sure. Nor was I sure I liked it—but I knew better than to argue. If she told me to sit, I sat.

She returned moments later. She handed me the lemonade and then settled into her seat. The seat from which she ran her fiefdom. She ruled her roost—and I loved her for it. Had made things easier when I needed help. She never batted an eyelash at offering me whatever I needed. I'd stayed here while I went to college. Then Trey stayed.

Nana was the best woman I knew.

"Now, young man, what's up?"

At forty-two, I'd never felt less like a young man. I toed the carpet with my boot. The boot I should've removed. That she hadn't said anything spoke volumes to her understanding of my inner turmoil.

She narrowed her gaze. "You've met someone."

I should've been surprised, but I wasn't. She knew everything about me—or at least she thought she did.

"Who is the young man? Do you have a picture?"

My breath caught as my eyes widened.

She waved me off. "Aaron, I've known you were gay for years. But you never said anything, so I respected your privacy. And before you ask, Trey never said a word. Shared with me that he's...heteroflexible...but we never talked about you."

"I... Uh..." I'd never purposefully kept this from my grandmother. There'd never been a guy, so why go down that path? "You don't mind?"

She narrowed her gaze. "You know, that's almost an offensive question. But it would've bothered your mother, and your asshole father certainly would've tried to beat it out of you."

This I'd known.

"There's a guy…"

"Yes." She sat a little straighter. "What's his name?"

"Noel."

"How did you meet him?"

"Well, that's a funny story." Which I recounted. I left out the hand and blow jobs, but I shared the rest. My heart ached by the time I finished the story.

"And he's been gone two weeks?"

"Yes, Nana."

"And what have you done in the past two weeks? To advance the relationship?"

"He made it pretty clear he didn't want a relationship."

She scowled.

I lived in dread of that scowl. "Uh, apparently not enough. I don't even have his phone number or address."

"But his sister lives a few blocks from you." She tapped her thigh. "Seems to me you know what to do."

"He's in Canada."

"When has something like geography ever stopped you?"

I couldn't think of a time when geography hadn't been an issue, but I knew better than to argue with Nana. "What about you? Trey? The inn?"

"Seems to me there's a young woman looking for a job. Something tells me she'd do well in a structured environment, and you can certainly guide her from afar. And your staff practically run the place. If she takes care of guests, your place will be just fine."

Stunned. I'd never considered giving Kendra a job…and yet Nana had a point. Kendra thrived being around people, and that was the bulk of my job. Cecelia did the staffing roster, and my bookkeeper kept the financing in order. Jason managed the front desk and trained any new staff we took on. Rocco, our chef, ran the kitchen the way he wanted, and I'd been thinking of promoting Kat to manager for a while now. They were young, but they also had a talent for keeping things moving.

Could I do this? Was it really that simple? "He might not want me."

"Bullshit."

Stunned.

Again.

"Could you, uh, repeat that?"

"I said, bullshit." She offered a serene smile.

But I felt the steel in my guts.

"You've put everyone ahead of yourself for too damn long. Why not do this? Okay, so he may not want you. Or he's been up in Canada pining for you. And sure, you may make a fool of yourself. So what? You come back here, and we take care of you. Maybe you find something other than work to occupy your time. Try a hobby. Like, I don't know, woodworking or something?"

The idea was almost too absurd to contemplate.

Almost.

But Nana was the wisest woman I knew. Correction, wisest person I knew.

And, deep in my heart, I knew she was right. If I didn't go to Canada and tell Noel how I really felt, I'd never have peace.

I left Nana's a few hours later with renewed purpose.

First, I had a heart-to-heart with Trey. He wasn't interested in taking over Cataluma Inn, despite his business training. He mentioned he was looking into something with Mateo.

I warned him I might not be able to back him financially.

He said that was fine.

But I kept in the back of my mind that I could always sell the house.

I had a long heart-to-heart with Kendra.

To say she was excited was an understatement. She confided she and Javier had decided to wait a bit to start a family and that she really wanted to work.

Miriam was working with her to get all the paperwork arranged, and she should be able to start working shortly. In the meantime, she was happy to job shadow everyone to get a feel for what went on in the inn. She confided that, in the end, she likely just needed structure—that all her previous attempts at a career had involved her trying to strike out on her own. As Noel had done. And although she had discipline, she also needed imposed structure.

Also, as I suspected, she loved the idea of working with the public. Her bubbly personality fit with the atmosphere of the inn, so I didn't have any concerns. She'd defer to Cecelia and Jason as she learned the ropes.

Both of my loyal employees made it clear they didn't want more responsibility. Jason was nearing retirement, and Cecelia had her sick brother at home. She needed to only be responsible when she was working, and didn't want to be on call or have added responsibilities.

Finally, Kat leapt at the chance to run front of house for the restaurant. Apparently, they'd had several ideas but had been hesitant to bring them up. Now, though, they felt confident.

I green-lit every one and then left them in charge.

Kendra provided me with her brother's contact information.

Still, I didn't call.

In the end, this had to be done in person.

If he rejected me, I needed to see his face when he did it.

That pretty much made me a masochist, but as I rode my motorcycle north with just a knapsack of clothes, a calm settled over me.

No matter what happened, I was going to be okay.

Chapter Seventeen

Noel

The sound of a motorcycle drew my attention. I sat at the dining-room table with my laptop open and papers spread everywhere. Normally, I worked in my home office. This morning I needed to put things out where I could see them visually, so this table was the only logical choice.

When the doorbell rang, I startled. No one ever came here. Well, except Lionel and April, and they both had keys and knew my open-door policy during work hours. At ten o'clock on a Friday morning, they wouldn't ring the bell.

Unless they forgot their keys.

Okay, fair enough.

I trudged to the door, unlocked it, and swung it open.

All the air in my lungs whooshed out. Then I blinked. Several times.

Aaron waved. Then his smile fell a little.

Damn.

"Come in. Please." I stood aside so he could enter.

I reached for his helmet, and he handed it over.

After placing it on the sofa, I indicated the backpack.

He eyed the sofa. "Everything's covered in dust. Oregon was pretty dry."

I didn't doubt it. We hadn't had a speck of rain up here either since I'd returned from Cataluma. "I don't care. Honestly, I don't give a shit. But if I don't give you a hug in the next thirty seconds, I might not believe you're real." I didn't bother to ask how he'd known to find me. Undoubtedly my sister'd been only too happy to give up my whereabouts.

We'd settled into an uneasy peace. I'd shipped her clothes and a few sentimental family heirlooms to California—along with a wedding present.

She'd sent back a flurry of emojis in a text.

Pretty much all was back to normal.

Aaron handed over the backpack, and I put it carefully on the leather couch.

The one I could easily wipe down later.

Then he crouched to undo his laces.

Oh, my God, I thought I'd lose my mind. I needed to touch him. To kiss him. To feel his heartbeat—to know this was real.

Finally, when he finished removing his boots, he stood before me.

I opened my arms.

He stepped into them.

The hug was crushing.

I didn't care.

How long we stood like that, I wasn't certain.

All the stress of the past month slowly melted away. He was here. I hadn't slept with Anderson. Weirdly, that was the thought that popped into my head. How I'd feel now if I had taken the man to bed.

Oh, for fuck's sake, get over yourself.

Yes. I should focus on what was before me, not some hypothetical that'd never happened.

He pulled back, only to gaze into my eyes.

I read the desire.

When he moved in for a kiss, I was happy to reciprocate.

Tongues parried. Teeth clashed.

His hand slid down my back to cup my ass. Holding me in place, he thrust against me.

My cock sat up and took notice.

Still, I pulled back. "You must be exhausted."

He shook his head. "Took me three days to get here. I made it to Bellingham last night. I didn't want to try crossing the border that late and, uh, I wasn't sure if you might have company—"

I pressed my finger to his lips. "No company. No one. Just you." I wanted to say forever, but I still wasn't sure how long he was planning to stay. Maybe this was just a visit. A lovely surprise, to be sure, but perhaps not a forever kind of thing.

"Am I interrupting your work?"

"What work?"

He smiled at my impish comeback. Then he took in my outfit. "Jeans? A T-shirt?"

"Well, it's not a hot day. And I try to go casual on Fridays. I don't have any meetings, so I didn't feel like dressing up."

"I didn't know you knew what casual was."

I tweaked his nose. "You're a funny one."

"In a good way or a bad way?"

"Uh, always in a good way. I'd never make fun of you—surely you know that by now."

He held my gaze. "I'm not sure of a lot of things right now."

Ah.

"Well, let me clear some up. *Mi casa es su casa.* That's the expression, right? I might've fucked it up."

"I know what you mean." Still, his face carried caution with that little v in his forehead.

"I have a spare room you can have or—even better—you can share mine with me."

His brow unknit. "Yeah, I'd really like that."

"And you can stay as long as you like. As long as you can. As long as—"

This time, he placed a finger to my lips. "Let's take it day by day." He cleared his throat. "I'm here on a visitor's visa. I'm applying for a work permit."

"You don't need to work."

He drew a breath.

"No, you really don't. I make enough to support us. Plus, don't you have a business in California? You can't just—"

There went the finger to the lips again.

"Kendra's running the inn for now."

I could've sworn that my eyes bugged out of my head. Kendra? My wayward sister? The one who never took anything seriously? He trusted her?

Yet even as I had the unspoken thoughts, I saw the serenity in his eyes. Whatever had led him to this decision, he was comfortable with it.

"And you're worried about being bored?"

"I'm worried about feeling like a kept man."

In my heart, I knew what the solution was. "If we get married, they'll expedite your work permit."

Holy shit, did I just say that?

Yes. Yes, I did.

I expected panic, but I only saw a softening in his expression.

"You took the words out of my mouth. Well, it's right that you do it because it's your life I'll be upending—"

"I think moving from California to Canada constitutes upending your life as well."

"Nevertheless, I don't have the right to expect you to simply accommodate me."

"Oh, I'll accommodate the shit out of you. You're going to be so accommodated—so pampered—that you're never going to want to leave."

He offered a small smile. "You really don't need time to think about this?"

I shook my head with vehemence. "I've just spent the most miserable month of my life trying to figure out how to move to California and worrying you'd reject me and then where would I be?"

"You'd have done it?"

"For you? I'd do anything."

He must've read the sincerity in my eyes, because he pressed our lips together.

The kiss was reverential. Holy, almost. A sealing of a promise with the sealing of lips.

Which turned into a hot, sexy kiss that left me breathless.

"You must be hungry."

His grin was sheepish. "Yeah, I didn't eat this morning—too nervous."

"Well, let's go to Fifties. You can order a huge breakfast, if you like. Or a burger. Or steak. Or any other of dozens of items."

He held up his hands. "An order of pancakes would be perfect."

"With whipped cream, a side of blueberries and bacon, of course."

"Yeah, okay. Canadian bacon or—"

"You can pick. Or have both."

He licked his lips. "Both sounds good."

And since I'd had only a slice of toast five hours ago, food sounded appetizing as well. I hadn't had a decent meal in...not counting fast food? About four weeks.

"I'll show you where the bathroom is." I snagged his backpack. "And my bedroom."

He grinned, his eyes shining bright. "Oh, that's a room I hope we see a lot of."

"Sure. Or the living room, dining room, kitchen, bathroom...and I have a media room downstairs. Oh." I grinned wickedly. "I've always had this vague dream of getting a blow job while I'm working at my desk."

"Where's the desk? We could do that fantasy right now."

We didn't. I coaxed him into getting changed and then we took my SUV down to Fifties. He ordered everything I'd suggested while I opted for a burger and chocolate shake. Best burger in Mission City, I contended. Well, perhaps the best in British Columbia.

When we got home, clearly Aaron was flagging. I convinced him to put his motorcycle in my garage, and then I coaxed him to undress and get into bed.

He wanted to give me a hand job.

I shed my clothes, climbed in next to him, and held him in my arms.

He was asleep in minutes.

Should I leave him to sleep?

Nah.

I had a million things to do—including figuring out how to get us married as quickly as possible—but everything could wait. I still couldn't believe he was here. In my house. In my arms.

And I knew, without a shadow of a doubt, that everything'd be okay.

When he awoke, some time later, we exchanged hand jobs. Again, I wasn't sure if our relationship would ever progress to more, and it didn't fucking matter. We were together. That was all that counted.

Over a dinner of takeout Chinese—because I had nothing worth cooking in the house—we planned out our future. A few google searches helped us figure out the quickest way to marry. Immigration likely wouldn't be thrilled, but the lawyer I hired, Arnav Sankar, had plenty of good advice.

We made a shopping list of everything we needed to buy.

We called Kendra to let her know.

She offered to ship Aaron's things up here.

After a bit, we accepted her offer.

Apparently things were going well at the inn.

On the list of everything to buy, I included a helmet.

Aaron cocked his head.

"Well, you plan to take me on your motorcycle, right? And we'll need to buy you a car for the winter. Snow's a thing up here."

He blinked several times.

I smiled.

When we retired to bed, we gave each other blow jobs.

Three days later, with a Marriage Commissioner officiating, we married in my backyard. Somehow, Anderson, his daughter, Shaw, and Shaw's fiancé Damien attended along with Damien's twin daughters, Sedona and Paget. Lionel and April were there as well. Oh, and my father.

That'd been Aaron's doing.

Seemed the crazy man had called my father and sought permission to marry me.

I'd never heard of anything so ludicrous.

Thank God, my father'd agreed. I still wasn't sure what I would've done if he'd said *no*.

After the ceremony, we got an enormous table at White Spot and had a celebration dinner. Somehow, this weird conglomeration of people had become *my* people.

Somewhere in there, Aaron took over management of the Grand Hotel and was overseeing the desperately needed renovations, I negotiated a contract to do marketing for Shaw's company, Damien promised to find a good used car for Aaron, and we did a video call with Kendra, Javier, and Trey.

I managed to suss out that Javier's mother, the mayor, had not reappeared, and some guy named Harold had taken over. Apparently this was all the town was talking about. Oh, and the five new couples who'd gotten together in the last few months. Wedding bells abounded.

Trey and I did a private chat to discuss the money I'd gifted him to buy his share of Diego's garage. Apparently the sale had gone through, and everything looked great.

As the evening drew to a close, Aaron and I thanked our guests.

To my surprise, Shaw handed us our helmets.

I glanced at Aaron.

He smiled sheepishly.

Damien laughed. "Aaron asked me to ride his bike down here and to keep it secret." He pointed to the helmets. "So you can ride off into the sunset."

Well, we were headed to Vancouver for a night before heading over to Vancouver Island for a honeymoon. A few days spent exploring B.C.'s capital had been Aaron's request. He wanted to see all of my home.

I hefted the backpack Damien had also brought. Then I put on my new helmet.

Aaron mounted the motorcycle.

I hopped onto the back.

He'd given me plenty of instructions, and we weren't taking the highway this evening.

After giving me one last look—and me giving him the thumbs-up—we said goodbye to our friends.

And drove off into the sunset.

Did you read Javier and Kendra's book? Grab *High on Love* here!

Curious about Anderson? Check out his book!
Anderson's Reinvention

Want more Gabbi Grey?
Check out her Love in Mission City series, set in beautiful British Columbia.

The first book is
Ginger Snapping All the Way (Love in Mission City Book 1)

Also available:

Stanley's Christmas Redemption(Love in Mission City Book 2)

The Beauty of the Beast (Love in Mission City Book 2.5)

Sleigh Bells and Second Chances (Love in Mission City Book 3)

Rayne's Return (Love in Mission City Book 4)

Gideon's Gratitude (Love in Mission City Book 5)

Quinton's Quest (Love in Mission City Book 6)

Ulysses's Ultimatum (Love in Mission City Book 7)

Love in Mission City: The Four Seasons

Love in Mission City: The Boyfriend Gamble

Love in Mission City: The Boyfriends Duet

Love in Mission City: The Shorts

Love in Mission City: The Boyfriends Duet

Rayne Check

Archer's Awakening

Leo's Lust

Finn's Find

Styx's Storm

A Daddy for Christmas 2: Foster

Puppy Pride

A Daddy for Christmas 3: Lorcan

Pup, Pup, and Away

A Daddy for Christmas 4: Raphael

Thought You Were the One

Love Without Reservations

Page Against the Machine
The Lightkeeper's Love Affair
Ace's Place
Marcus's Cadence
Not in it for the Money

Also:

Edging Coach (co-written with L.A. Witt)
Hugh (Single Dads of Gaynor Beach)
Anthony (Single Dads of Gaynor Beach)
Xavier (Single Dads of Gaynor Beach)
Love Furever (Friends of Gaynor Beach Animal Rescue)
Husky Love (Friends of Gaynor Beach Animal Rescue)
Yorkie to My Heart (Friends of Gaynor Beach Animal Rescue)
A Furever Home (co-written with Kaje Harper – Friends of Gaynor
Beach Animal Rescue)
Axe to Grind (Road to Rocktoberfest 2023)
Grindstone's Edge (Road to Rocktoberfest 2024)
Voice to Raise (Road to Rocktoberfest 2025)
Drums and Lullabies (Road to Rocktoberfest 2026)
My Past, Your Future
If Only for Today
Catch a Tiger by the Tail
Solstice Surprise
Valentino in Vancouver
You See Me
Sun, Surf, and Surprises
Ginger in the City
Caressa's Homecoming (Bound by Love Book 1)

Cole's Reckoning (Bound by Love Book 2)

Donovan's Men (Bound by Love Book 3)

A Little Christmas: Tobias

Sizzling Sydney Nights

An Uncommon Gentleman

A Sensible Gentleman

A Wounded Gentleman

Didn't See You Coming

Finding Noah (Foggy Basin Season 2)

Noah's Holiday (A Foggy Basin Short Story)

Dancing Through Pride (A Foggy Basin Short Story)

Keystrokes and Kittens (Foggy Basin Season 3)

Hot Rucking Canadian

Big Rucking Disaster

Unlocked and Unlost

Audiobooks

Ginger Snapping All the Way

Stanley's Christmas Redemption

Sleigh Bells and Second Chances

Rayne's Return

Gideon's Gratitude

Quinton's Quest

Ulysses's Ultimatum

Rayne Check

Archer's Awakening

Leo's Lust

Finn's Find

A Daddy for Christmas 2: Foster
Puppy Pride
A Daddy for Christmas 3: Lorcan
Thought You Were the One
Love in Mission City: The Shorts
Page Against the Machine
The Lightkeeper's Love Affair
Ace's Place
Marcus's Cadence
Not in it for the Money
Hugh (Single Dads of Gaynor Beach)
Anthony (Single Dads of Gaynor Beach)
Love Furever (Friends of Gaynor Beach Animal Rescue)
Husky Love (Friends of Gaynor Beach Animal Rescue)
A Furever Home (co-written with Kaje Harper – Friends of Gaynor
Beach Animal Rescue)
My Past, Your Future
If Only for Today
Catch a Tiger by the Tail
Solstice Surprise
An Uncommon Gentleman
A Sensible Gentleman
A Wounded Gentleman
Didn't See You Coming
Unlocked and Unlost

Want a free short story? The story is set in Gaynor Beach, California where there are plenty of single dads and puppy rescues! You can sign up for my newsletter so you can keep up with all the great stuff I'm doing as well as pictures of my own pooches, Ally and Finnegan.

Hemingway's Happy Day

Love contemporary MF romances? What's better than love in the beautiful Cedar Valley in British Columbia, Canada? Find small town romances with a touch of angst, a bit of heat, and a lot of heart...

The Absolution of Abigail Reardon (prequel)

The Luminosity of Loriana Harper (Book 1)

The Making of Marnie Jones (Book 2)

The Redemption of Remy St. Claire (Book 3)

Interested in knowing more about Gabbi?

Sign up for her newsletter

Follow her on Bookbub

Follow her on Instagram

USA Today Bestselling author Gabbi Grey lives in beautiful British Columbia where her fur baby chin-poo keeps her safe from the nasty neighborhood squirrels. Working for the government by day, she spends her early mornings writing contemporary, gay, sweet, and dark erotic BDSM romances. While she firmly believes in happy endings, she also believes in making her characters suffer before finding their true love. She also writes m/f romances as Gabbi Black and Gabbi Powell.